DEMON DOWN

XOE MEYERS - BOOK FOUR

SARA C. ROETHLE

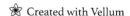

PROLOGUE

I came back out with my oversized Edgar Allan Poe mug filled with coffee and lots of cream. Allison and Lucy had made Max move to the love seat with Chase so they could sit together on the couch and save me a spot between them.

I sat down and took my first sip of coffee. Feeling instantly better I asked, "Aren't you all sick of me yet?"

"Don't be silly Xoe," Max answered. "You're our wise and omnipotent benefactor."

I threw a pillow at him, almost spilling my coffee in the process. I had a feeling I'd be hearing jokes about me being their new leader for quite some time.

The front door opened again to reveal Jason, freshly scrubbed and dressed in a flannel shirt and jeans. I liked the flannel way better than the dress clothes.

Before he could walk in, a fire erupted momentarily behind him, quickly extinguishing to reveal my dad.

Jason was unfazed by my dad's abrupt appearance. He simply walked inside then held the door for him.

My dad looked unusually disheveled. He was normally the picture of good hygiene, but now his gray dress shirt was missing a few buttons and had one sleeve torn off, and his face and clothing were covered either in ash or dirt.

He straightened his collar and cleared his throat. "This Bartimus problem might be a bigger deal than I originally thought."

1

My dad huffed and picked at the frayed sleeve of his dress shirt. "Bunch of barbarians," he mumbled as he switched to dusting off his charcoal gray slacks. His usually perfect blonde hair was a total mess, falling forward to partially cover his green eyes that perfectly matched my own.

"Um . . . " I began nervously as I stood. "Care to explain what you're doing in my house?"

My dad met my eyes. "That little deal you made has backfired astronomically," he explained.

I glared at him. "You know I didn't have a choice, so spare me the lecture and tell me what happened."

He strode further into the room and took a seat on the now vacant couch. "Is your mother home?" he asked casually, though I knew the answer was more important than he let on.

I sighed. "No. You're at no risk of having anything thrown at you . . . at least not by her," I amended.

My dad sighed in return, and turned features that looked startlingly similar to mine to face me. "I was doing some research into the claims you made to Bartimus," he explained. "When I was attacked by several half-demon lackeys. Of course, they could have just politely informed me that their masters wanted to be able to go above ground as well, but *no*. Hence, they all had to die."

Just a few days before, I had made a deal with the demon Bartimus, Bart for short. Now, it's basically rule number one to never make deals with demons, but I really had no choice. You would think since I was a half-demon myself, it wouldn't be a big deal, but it was. I had been thoroughly lectured on my actions. Never mind that Chase and I would likely be dead if I hadn't made the deal.

I highly doubted that the deal would even come to fruition regardless. Bart wanted to walk in the human world, but he had no human blood and was therefore physically incapable of doing so. My dad only had a tiny trace of human blood, but it was enough to allow him to travel freely.

I had promised to help Bart find a loophole, or else I would end up his errand girl. I don't know why Bart even thought me capable of carrying through on the act of freeing him. Sure, I have some demon powers, but my control over them is pathetic at best.

At the last moment my dad had swooped in and done

the actual signing of the contract, making him the one actually indebted to Bart, but I was still getting all of the blame.

My mouth was gaping in surprise at my dad's words. Well, at the killing all of the half-demons part. Though I knew he was fully capable, it was still difficult to imagine my dad killing anyone.

The rest of my friends present: Chase, Jason, Max, Lucy, and Allison, all kept their distance during our exchange, unsure of what this new event meant for us.

"How did they find out!" I asked as my brain finally processed everything. The only people who knew about the deal were in my living room, besides Bart of course.

My dad rolled his eyes. "Bart has always been a gossip. I should have seen it coming, really. I just thought he would be smart enough to not want to hinder our search in any way. The other demons knowing about the deal makes things complicated. More complicated than they were before, at least."

"Maybe he believed it would make us work faster," Chase chimed in as he stepped forward, effectively including himself in the conversation. "A little added incentive."

Besides me and my father, Chase was the only other person in the room with demon blood. He was also the only other person in the room that my dad would pay any mind to. Most demons seemed to have an extreme superiority complex. Non-demons only matter as long as they're useful. I knew that Chase didn't share in those archaic views, but sometimes I wasn't so sure about my father.

My dad nodded at Chase's suggestion thoughtfully. "That probably was his convoluted plan, yes, but he is wrong."

"Well we weren't going to let him out anyway, right?" I asked, needing reassurance.

My dad snorted. "We're contractually bound to try, so try we will. There might be a way . . . " he trailed off, "if we are able to release him, then we can just kill him afterward. It would simplify matters a great deal. It's likely not possible either way, but I signed a contract obligating me to at least try . . . and," he paused.

"And?" I prompted.

"And Bart believes there is a way," he said. "There has to be a reason for it. Why now? He has existed nearly one thousand years. Why does he now think there is a loophole, unless it has something to do with you?"

"Me?" I asked. "Why would I have anything to do it?"

My dad shifted on the couch to face me better. "Think about it. I have known Bart for a very long time. If he thought I had the means to release him, he would have attempted to blackmail me into a contract sooner. The only thing that has changed . . . is you. I do not think that Bart working with that vampire was a coincidence. I think he found her, not the other way around."

The vampire in question had been named Maggie. She was the one that turned Jason into a vampire, and she had taken an instant dislike to me. Maybe because I set her on fire once or twice. It wasn't like she didn't have it coming. In the end she made it clear that one of us had to die, and well, I'm still here.

I shook my head. I wasn't liking where my dad was going with his line of conversation. "And what would happen if we just, you know, broke the contract?" I asked.

My dad gave me a look like I was being silly. "Demons may not have much of a community," he explained. "But if I were to break that contract, I would be hunted down and tortured for a good long while. Eventually they would kill me, but only once I begged for it. We take our contracts very seriously."

I sipped my previously forgotten coffee while I thought about the situation. Its cool temperature made it taste bitter, but I continued drinking it anyway.

"So," I began as I continued to think, "we'll do the research, which will ultimately be fruitless. It has to be. If Bart thinks there is anything special to me, then he's mistaken. We put on a good show with research, then we're off the hook."

My dad sighed. "Not quite. As you recall, you also included in your deal that if you could not find a loophole, you would become Bart's personal errand girl. As I took over the contract for you, that responsibility would fall to me. I fear even I would have trouble stomaching the acts that Bartimus would request of me."

"So we kill him," I said simply.

My dad laughed, but not like it was funny. "It is not quite so easy as all of that," he explained. "Bart does not leave his lair often, and he definitely will not risk it now. His powers are of the mind, therefore he does not fair well around other demons whose powers are of a more physical nature. In his lair he is in control and could trap even the most strong-willed demon with his illusions. We would not stand a chance against him."

"Ok," Max interrupted.

My dad stood and looked down at him, and with the nine inch height difference (Max is only 5'4"), my dad had to look down a long way.

Max seemed nonplussed as he pushed his sandy blond hair away from his freckled face. "I have to know. You demons are always talking about lairs and *underground*. Do demons seriously just like, live in an underground cave system or something?"

My dad glared at Max, but answered, "Not quite. Demons reside in a different reality. Our reality mostly intermingles with this one, but not entirely. The demon reality is limited to a smaller space, and most of that space is underground in both realities."

"Oh," Max answered with a confused look on his face.

I didn't blame him. It confused me too. "So what do we do then?" I asked. "If we can't kill him in his lair, and we can't free him, then kill him . . . "

My dad eyed me very steadily, making sure that I would listen to every word he had to say. "Our aim is to free him so that we might kill him. If there is even the slightest possibility that it might work . . . until then we must go to ground, Alexondra. We must hide away. If we cannot free him, eventually he will be forced to come to us for the answers he seeks. If we can free him, we need to remain alive long enough to do so."

I laughed, then realized my dad was not at all joking. "We can't go to ground!" I shouted, slopping cold coffee all over my hand.

"We are too vulnerable here," he explained. "Or do you not recall the alternate reality that Bart so easily put you into just a few short days ago?"

"But I escaped-" I began.

My dad tsked at me. "You escaped because he left you an escape hatch. The end result was always for you to end up in his lair where Maggie waited. Where *he* waited. And there is something else. I've been thinking about how Bart was able to trap you in the first place. He should not have been able to do it without some of your blood. He can't just snatch demons into his lair by sheer force of will alone."

"My blood?" I questioned weakly.

He nodded. "Whereas witches can partially summon a demon to this realm, a demon can also be summoned back underground. Using that demon's blood allows for a complete summoning. The demon would be pulled underground entirely, leaving nothing in this realm. Using your blood would have been the only way for Bart to bring you to his lair. Now Xoe, can you think of any way that he might have gotten your blood."

I thought for a moment and began to shake my head, but stopped. Not long ago I had been kidnapped by a group of witches and a werewolf named Nick. Not only had I been unconscious long enough for them to take blood without me knowing if they so chose, but they had been working with a demon. We never knew for sure what demon it was.

My kidnapper's goal had been to kill supernaturals and steal their powers using their blood, which wasn't actually possible. Yet if a demon had powers of illusion, he could make them *think* it was possible. Perhaps the demon wasn't just causing chaos for the fun of it, and was in reality just after the blood . . .

"Ruh Roh," I squeaked as Bart's plot came together in my mind.

"What is it Scooby?" Max asked worriedly.

"I think Bart was the demon working with Nick and the witches," I explained. "He tricked them into killing supernaturals and used his illusions to make them believe that they would get their powers. Once their confidence had been bolstered, he sent them after a demon. He sent them after *me*."

I thought back to the night that Nick had planned on killing me. We were in the woods. He summoned the demon that wanted my blood, but my dad had stopped Nick before he could kill me.

What if Bart had never planned on Nick killing me? Bart could have tricked the witches into giving him some of my blood before the whole scene had even gone down. It had never made sense that the witches thought they could steal powers, but Bart could make them believe anything.

"He wanted your blood," my dad said, instantly understanding. "That night in the woods," he went on, "the demon left as soon as I arrived, not because he was afraid, but because he knew I would save you. He knew his job was done. Bart has had your blood all along, and was just waiting for the right moment."

"But then why did he ask for my blood when I was trapped in his lair?" I countered.

My dad let out a frustrated breath. "More blood equals more control. He would have drained you close to death given the chance."

My mouth went dry, and I couldn't seem to manage a full breath. Jason came to my side and pulled me close to him. "I will go with you," he said steadily, accepting things for what they were.

My dad shook his head. "There is no need to involve others in this. It is demon business."

My vampire boyfriend glared at my father, but didn't reply.

"Anyone could be a target," I countered shakily. "Just because I'm the only one that Bart can summon doesn't mean someone can't just send half-demons after everyone else. We can't just leave them up here."

"Bart cannot directly target anyone that is not near you," my dad explained. "He was only able to entrap Max and Chase because they were with you. You being near them puts them all in harm's way. A human or a werewolf would have to summon Bart for interaction otherwise."

I shook my head, not wanting to believe what he was telling me, but knowing that it was the truth. "He could still send half-demons after them," I repeated.

My father seemed to think for a moment. "Abel will be obligated to protect them," he said finally. "It was announced to the pack that you are his. It would be very bad for him if something was to happen to your pack, especially after he had been alerted to the danger."

"But-" I began.

"No," my dad interrupted. "I've let you endanger yourself far too much already."

I glared at him. "Mom will never let me go underground with you."

My dad took a deep breath in and let it out slowly. "Your mother will not risk your life just to keep you away from me. She stands no chance of protecting you."

"What about her!" I shouted. "Abel will protect the members of our pack, but mom isn't part of that."

"Then she will come with us," he said simply.

My jaw dropped. "She won't even be in the same room with you," I argued. "She'll never go for it."

My dad began to pace. "I will speak with her," he said finally.

"That's not a good idea," I said, but I was talking to empty air. My dad had disappeared in a puff of smoke, presumably to find my mother.

I sat down on the couch in an attempt to stop my head

from spinning. I didn't remember agreeing to it, but somehow plans had been made for us to go to ground. Well, for Chase and me at least. I knew there was no way Jason would let me go without him, and I wouldn't want to, so he was coming too . . . and my mom. This was a very bad idea.

I'd been worried about Bart before, but now with the possibility of this all being some part of a master plan . . . I was terrified. For him to go to all of this trouble, he really had to believe that I was the only one who could help him escape. I had a feeling that my dad knew more about Bart's thoughts than he was telling me. If there was some way for me to free Bart, my dad would know about it, wouldn't he?

Lucy pulled her cell phone out of her pocket. She had been silent the entire time my dad was present, but her attention never faltered as she took in all of the facts.

"I'm going to call Lela," she announced as she walked across the room with Max following behind her. A moment after she disappeared into the kitchen I could hear her talking on her phone.

I sighed and shook my head. Just the fact of how readily my friends accepted the situation proves what a rough few months we'd all had. Emergency mode had become the norm.

Allison sat down on the couch beside me and pawed at the ends of her long blonde hair nervously. She bit her lip as if debating on what she was going to say. "I know you're probably processing a lot," she began slowly, "but what am I supposed to do?"

I smiled at her weakly. I could probably talk Abel into watching over her as well, but that would put her around more werewolves again. I knew for a fact that she still intended on becoming one, so leaving her with the pack would be a recipe for disaster.

She could stay in Shelby away from the werewolves, but what was to stop some half-demon from snatching her and using her as a bargaining chip. There were too many risks to consider.

"You're coming with us," I decided.

"But your dad didn't seem to want-" she began.

"I don't care," I interrupted.

Allison glared at me. "You just don't want to leave me alone with whomever Abel brings to protect Lucy, Max, and Lela."

"That's exactly right," I agreed. "And you're not going to argue with me, because you know at the moment I have much bigger fish to fry."

Allison huffed. "At least I'll get to see the demon underworld," she replied dejectedly.

I nodded. "Yes Allison, at least there is that."

"I suppose we should repack," Jason added as he took a seat on my other side. His dark blue eyes betrayed the worry he was attempting to hide with a smile.

I looked up at Chase, the only one left standing. He ran his fingers through his near-black hair and shrugged.

"All of my worldly possessions are in a duffel bag. I'm ready when you are."

I sighed. "Will you go with Allison to pack her things?"

Chase nodded and turned to Allison. "Are your parents okay with you bringing . . . people home?" he asked.

Allison shrugged. "They're in Barbados or something. They didn't even know I went to Utah."

Chase raised his eyebrows, but didn't say anything. Without another word Allison stood and the two of them walked out the front door.

Jason and I sat in silence. I had no idea what he was thinking. I, on the other hand, was imagining what the confrontation would be like when my dad tried to tell my mom that we were all going on a little vacation into the land of the demons.

I knew she'd never go for it. My mom had not taken the news about the existence of supernatural beings well. Our relationship had deteriorated into casual pleasantries, and that was when we were even speaking at all.

She was apparently too afraid to ask about any of the details of my life anymore, which was a big change from how things used to be. I mean, my mom had always been more of a friend than a motherly figure, but now she didn't even feel like a friend. It gave me a much looser leash as far as what I could and couldn't do, but I'd take our old relationship and a few more rules any day of the week.

"We should pack," Jason announced, startling me out of my thoughts. He looked concerned and impatient, but didn't say anything else.

I nodded and stood to go upstairs with Jason following at my heels. Each step felt belabored as I walked up the stairs and into my room to pack yet again. Jason shut the door gently behind him as he followed me towards my bed. The suitcase I had taken to Utah was still packed and leaning the wall near my door. It had been so nice to be home . . . for all of two seconds.

With a sigh I lifted the suitcase and dumped the dirty clothes out onto my bed. The fancy dresses I'd brought toppled out along with my more comfortable clothes. Now that I no longer needed to play dress-up with were-wolves, I could get rid of the offending silky, glittery pieces of fabric. Of course, I'd eventually have to go to another coalition meeting and I might need the dresses again. The thought gave me a shiver. The time we'd spent in Utah had been a rough few days.

I picked out the clothes I would actually want to wear again and let the dresses topple to the floor. Everything was dirty, and one or two things had blood stains. Like I said, a rough few days. I wondered if I'd have time to do a load of laundry before we had to leave. I really didn't have that many clothes, and most of them were now lying dirty on my bed.

"I wonder if my dad has a washing machine," I said out loud.

Jason shrugged. "Everything that's going on . . . and

that's what you're thinking about?" I shrugged in response, and he added, "He has to wash his clothes somehow."

I laughed and it felt strange. "It just seems so . . . mundane." I turned to face him. "What if it takes more than a week?"

It took Jason a moment to catch up with my train of thought. "First laundry, and now you're worried about school?" he asked.

I scoffed. "It's the second half of Junior year. I *so* did not suffer in that hell-hole for this long, just to drop out to go to another quite literal hell-hole."

"Is it really that important?" he asked.

It took me a moment to close my gaping jaw. "Just because you never went to high school, doesn't mean that it isn't important," I replied.

Jason was born a human in 1883. Prep schools and such had existed back then, but they weren't so much an *every teenager must go here or else* kind of thing. He'd had no traditional education to speak of, but he'd still had plenty of time to acquire knowledge. I wasn't going to be challenging him to a math-off any time soon.

Jason smiled. "Perhaps Lucy can pick up your home-work for you. We all know she won't be missing school no matter how many half-demons are after her."

I smiled. He was right, Lucy didn't even miss school after she got scratched by a werewolf. "Do you think Abel will really send protection here for them?" I asked, then before he could answer I went on, "Can you send things to the demon underground? How will she get the homework to me after she picks it up?"

Jason put his hands on my shoulders and turned me around to sit on the bed. "Try not to worry about it right now," he said soothingly. "Your father will see to it."

Jason kissed me, just a soft brush of lips. I placed my hands on either side of his face and pulled him in for more. We ended up sitting close together with my head on his shoulder, just being still for a moment. It would have been nice to just spend a few days together, just the two of us. No werewolves, demons, or impending doom weighing on our relationship.

We'd had a little bit of time that way between me killing Dan, the guy that made Lucy a werewolf, and Lela showing up with Nick and begging me to be her werewolf pack leader. That had been a nice, quiet time, but it hadn't lasted very long. I could blame Nick for that. He was an all right guy if you could overlook the fact that he'd been in league with the band of witches that was killing supernatural beings in order to steal their powers. Knowing that Nick had been manipulated by Bart still didn't excuse his actions. Now Nick was dead. Just like Dan, and just like Maggie. I was beginning to see a trend.

I straightened and shook my head. I felt like maybe I should be crying, but I couldn't muster a single tear. Really, compared to everything else that had happened, hiding out for a little while wasn't even that bad. Considering that just a few days ago I had been immersed in werewolf politics, hunted by vampires, all while making deals with demons . . . well, this was a walk in the park. Yet, the idea of Bartimus thinking that I was somehow the key to his freedom had me on edge.

I stood and bundled my clothes into my arms to go downstairs to the washing machine. The underground could wait until I had clean clothes. Jason followed behind me, picking up fallen socks as I made my way back downstairs.

I had just started the water in the machine when my mom came barreling through the front door, fluttering her arms about like a crazed bird. "Absolutely not!" she shouted shrilly, not realizing that I was only a room away.

"Libby," my dad said patiently. "It is the only way. It's not safe for either of you to stay here a moment longer."

"I don't believe you Alexondre!" she shouted back. "You're just trying to manipulate us to-"

"Libby," my dad said calmly, interrupting her. "This is about the safety of our daughter, and your own safety as well."

"She is not *your* daughter," my mom spat back. "I've raised her by myself all of these years. You can't just waltz in here now and take her away. She wouldn't be in any danger if it wasn't for you. You-" she hesitated. "You made her a demon. She should have been normal."

I started to feel sick. I knew my mom didn't like the fact that I was a demon, but it still hurt that she wished I was something else, rather than just accepting what I am.

It was true that she had raised me by herself without any help from my father. Of course, she had left my dad and did her best to hide me from him. Still, my dad had found us, but didn't approach me until recently, when my powers manifested. My dad could continue to shoulder most of the blame as far as I was concerned, but they were really both to blame . . . at least a little.

I heard my dad sigh. "You'll need to come too. You could be used against her, and I do not believe that she's willing to leave you here."

"Xoe and I will leave town," my mom offered breathlessly. "We hid from you for all of these years. We can hide from this other . . . demon." She said the word like it was still unfamiliar on her tongue.

"He will find you almost instantly," my dad countered. "I promise you Libby. This is the only way."

Having had enough of eavesdropping I walked out into the living room. "We're going to have to wait for the washing machine to finish before we can go," I announced.

My mom ran to me and grabbed both of my hands in hers. "We can go anywhere you want Xoe," she offered, nearing on hysterics. "Just pick a place." Her dark brown eyes were red-rimmed and frantic. When she realized that she had grabbed me, she suddenly recoiled.

I felt near tears. She was afraid that I'd burn her. "It's not safe," I explained through gritted teeth. "We have to go with dad. It will only be for a little while."

My mom's eyes widened. "You're calling him dad?" she whispered.

I blushed. "Th-that's not really relevant right now," I stammered. "You need to go pack."

My mom looked down, then up again. "We'll do this," she said, "but once you're safe, we are going to move somewhere very far away."

I nodded. I didn't have the heart to tell her that I'd never be safe, even if we moved to Antarctica, I couldn't leave this life behind. I couldn't change what I was. No matter how hard I pushed things away, they would just come crashing back, like a boomerang from hell.

2

Chase and Allison walked through the still-open front door, drawing my attention away from my mom. They piled their luggage against the wall. Well, Allison piled her luggage, and Chase set down his one duffel bag.

"What is the human doing here?" my dad asked sharply. He was obviously riled from the conversation with my mom.

I rolled my eyes. "The *human* is coming with us. Just like mom, she's not pack and she could be a target."

My dad rolled his eyes right back at me. "Xoe, we cannot take every human you know. Humans are not supposed to be taken underground to begin with, let alone a vampire. We're already pushing it."

I put my hands on my hips and eyed him squarely. "Are we going or not?"

My dad bit his lower lip in annoyance, but answered

with a curt nod. "Pack quickly," he ordered. "I do not like being vulnerable."

"What about Lucy and Max?" I asked, they had snuck out sometime during the scene between my mother and father, and I hadn't had a chance to ask Lucy what Abel said when she'd called him.

My dad answered as he walked into the kitchen like he owned the place, "Abel has sent protection. They are not your concern anymore." A moment later the coffee grinder sounded. Maybe my mom wasn't the only one to blame for my coffee addiction either.

Chase came to stand beside me. He was dressed in his winter usual of a flannel shirt and worn jeans. His scruffy black hair fell nearly to his jaw. I on the other hand, though relatively scruffy-haired, was in a tank top and shorts. I hoped that my demonic hot-flashes ended soon. I seriously missed my comfy flannels. I shouldn't have had to deal with hot flashes for another thirty or forty years.

Like Chase, Allison was dressed warmly in a black sweater that made her honey blonde hair look white. She looked from me, to my mom, to Jason, who had just come down the stairs. Unsure of what to do, she finally shuffled over to the couch to sit and wait.

I spared a final reassuring look for my mom, though she didn't acknowledge it, then went to check on my clothes. I wished I hadn't started the laundry in the first place. It would have been nice to just get this whole big awkward moment over with. Now we would have to wait on the washer and dryer.

Chase walked into the laundry room as I was checking the dial on the washer. It still had a good fifteen minutes left. I leaned against the machine as I turned to face him, but Chase just stood there, not saying anything.

"Is there a reason that you're hovering?" I asked as I looked back at the washer again, willing the dial to move faster.

"I just-" he began, then stopped.

I turned back to face him. "Yes?" I prompted, giving him my full attention.

He opened his mouth to speak again, and the room suddenly shifted in front of my eyes. A look of concern crossed Chase's face just as I was overtaken by an immense feeling of vertigo.

"Are you-" Chase began.

The world shifted again. I pushed my hands back against the washing machine as I closed my eyes to steady myself. When I opened them I was somewhere else, and my hands pushed at empty air. There was a small wrought-iron café table set up in front of me. The table was in the middle of an expansive meadow, complete with wildflowers and a babbling brook. It would have been an idyllic scene, but the sky looked wrong somehow. It looked like it was made of something much more solid than the usual atmosphere. I looked back to the table just as an antique tea appeared on the table top. Crap.

Resigned, I took a seat just as Bartimus appeared and

sat in the other chair. The demon was as large as I remembered him, around 6'7" and half as wide as he was tall. Perfectly black eyes blended into his ink black skin. He grinned at me as he poured us each a cup of tea. The smell of rotted meat found its way to my nostrils, making me gag.

Bart's powers majored in illusion. He could create an entire new world in the blink of an eye, though it could come tumbling down just as easily. Regardless, I did not appreciate once again being trapped in such a world.

When he had trapped me before, the way out was simple. As soon as I realized I was in another reality, the reality fell away. Of course, Bart had wanted me to find my way out, just not as quickly as I had.

I knew this current reality was an illusion, yet it seemed pretty solid. Bart had managed to trap me in his lair with the last illusion. He had my blood and could therefore trap me whenever he wanted. I took a deep breath and tried to steady my pulse. I wasn't sure if I could handle another trip to Bart's lair.

"Have you made any progress on your promise my dear Alexondra?" he asked pleasantly. The undertone of menace was there, but I wasn't sure if it was intentional. I doubted that someone who looked and sounded like Bart could speak without menace even if they tried.

I took in a shallow breath through my mouth, but it did nothing to keep the rotten smell out of my sinuses. It seeped right in and took up camp in the back of my throat.

"We would be making more progress if we didn't have to worry about being attacked by half-demons at every turn," I answered.

Bartimus frowned. "Who would dare impede your research?"

I couldn't tell if his question was genuine or not. I was betting he was more in control of the situation than he'd have me believe.

I sighed and then gagged from the deep inhalation of breath. "Probably whatever demon you told about the deal," I managed to choke out.

The tea cup Bartimus was holding shattered in his massive hand. Rage washed over his face, then was suddenly gone. He didn't like being called a liar, even though he was one. "Well then we shall simply have to work faster, shall we not?" he asked, snarling his blocky, cracked teeth at me.

I glared at him. "Yes Bart, we shall."

What I wanted to say was, *no Bart, go back to the dark hole you belong in*, but I kept my mouth shut. Unfortunately Bart also has a knack for reading minds, a skill even more frightening than his illusions.

"I see you have figured a few things out, clever girl," he commented suddenly.

Crap, I had been thinking about the possibility of Bart being the demon in the woods to whom I was almost sacrificed, and if I'd still end up getting sacrificed at some point.

"So you confirm it then?" I asked. "You were the demon working with Nick?"

Bart smiled again, making my stomach acid curdle. "I do not confirm it, nor do I deny it."

"Whatever," I replied breathlessly. "You're going to need to send me back if you want me to work on our deal."

Bart eyed me thoughtfully, then suddenly we were in a graveyard that resembled the one we had in Shelby. I had very bad memories of that graveyard, and hated it at the best of times, but Bart had gone and made it a little worse.

I looked down at the graves of Lucy, Allison, Jason, and Chase. I didn't know why he'd omitted the other people in my life, but I did my very best not to think of them. Thinking of them could make them targets as well.

"I get the point," I stated coldly. I knew the graves were fake, but the threat was there.

Bart giggled, which was a strange sound to come from such a large demon. "I know *you* won't let me down Alexondra. You'll figure it out. Tick tock." He snapped his fingers.

I opened my eyes and sat straight up in bed. Bed? I looked around the room I was in. I didn't recognize it at all. The walls were paneled in dark wood on top of thick, dark blue carpeting. The bed I was in was one of those old-style four poster types. There was something strange about the room that I couldn't quite place, and then it hit me. The room had no windows. The light shining down on me was solely artificial. My heart dropped as I realized that I was in the demon underground. Where had Bart put me?

My ears were filled with the sound of my own frantic breathing. I took a few deep breaths, and was suddenly able to hear yelling in the next room. I slid out of bed and tip-toed up to the heavy wooden door, trying not to make any more sound than was necessary. I pushed the door open a crack and listened.

"What if she doesn't wake up!" my mom wailed.

"She will," my dad soothed. "Her body is here, which means he is only speaking to her. She cannot be harmed as long as we have her physically."

"But who is *he*?" my mom snapped. "Why would he have any interest in my daughter?"

My heart flooded with relief. I wasn't in Bart's lair after all. My parents were obviously safe, if not entirely getting along. My parents fighting about me meant that my friends were likely alive as well.

Chase's face appeared in front of the door, confirming my thoughts but also startling me. He grinned as I hopped back from the door in surprise. "Can I come in?"

I nodded and stepped away from the door. "Jason and Allison?" I questioned, just to make sure.

"Both here," Chase assured as he took a seat on the plain white bedspread.

"How long was I out?" I asked.

Only around fifteen minutes had gone by in Bart's illusion, but I knew that time could pass differently from one reality to another. From the sound of my mother's hysterics, I'd probably been gone awhile.

"A few hours," Chase answered. "As soon as we realized what had happened, your father insisted on bringing you down here. He said it would be more difficult for Bart to maintain the connection once you were underground. Something about not being able to summon you if you were already here."

I sat down beside Chase, feeling tired. "Bart is getting impatient," I explained. "Did Abel's people reach Shelby?"

Chase nodded. "Lucy and Max will be protected. They only have to worry about half-demons now. Without you near, Bart can't touch them."

I flopped back onto the bed, and Chase lowered himself down beside me. I turned my head to face him as I had a thought. "You were about to say something," I prompted, "before Bart came a'calling . . . "

Chase turned his gray eyes up to the ceiling. If I didn't know better, I'd say he was blushing. "Nothing of importance," he mumbled quietly.

I reached out an arm and shoved his shoulder. "I don't think so buddy," I chided. "Out with it."

Chase opened his mouth to speak, but then my mom came rushing into the room, followed by Jason and Allison. Chase closed his mouth and our eyes met for a moment before I was distracted by my mother.

Fresh tears stained her face that was already puffy from her previous tears. Her dark brown hair was a frizzy mess, and wafted around like tiny currents of air were tossing it about. She ran her fingers through it quickly, making it poof up even more. Jason gave me a strange look as he took in the sight of Chase and I lying on the bed.

I sat up and cleared my throat. "I'm fine," I said quickly as my mom approached me.

My mom nodded over and over and started crying again. Chase slid off the bed and made a hasty escape from the room as my mom and Jason closed in around me, expressing their worry. I watched him go, and envied his escape. Just a little.

3

The demon underground was not what I had expected. I had envisioned that everyone lived in dank, musty caves like Bartimus, but my dad had an actual house, as did many other demons. There was even a demon city of sorts, with demon streets and demon street signs. Chase and I were following my father down one such street.

The demons having a city in the underground made sense, since full-blooded demons were stuck unless summoned. The city was the central point that linked many of the demon abodes, though some demons like Bart chose to be a little more off the grid.

The city wasn't just populated by full demons either, as they're actually quite rare. Most demons have at least a small amount of human blood. I have slightly more than half, and Chase and my father have a lot less. Physically the three of us fit in just fine with humans, but that wasn't the case for all apparently. I noticed some demons with scales, and some with fur, and some that didn't even resemble humans in the slightest.

The different creatures intermingled as if their existence was entirely normal, and I suppose for them it was. I, on the other hand, was experiencing a bit of shell shock as I tried to take everything in at once. I caught Chase laughing at me more than a few times, and realized that he'd neglected to warn me on purpose.

"I'm glad this is entertaining for you," I sniped.

Chase simply grinned back at me and kept walking.

The three of us were on our way to the demon library. My mom, Allison, and Jason couldn't come into the city. Humans and vampires were persona non-grata in the demon world. They weren't even supposed to be in the underground at all, and therefore had to stay shut up inside my dad's house as long as we remained.

Chase began humming the Nutcracker Suite under his breath, completely at ease in our strange surroundings. Of course, he had grown up around demons, always knowing what he was and where he came from. So I got to be the only one who walked around gawking at our surroundings like a child experiencing an amusement park for the first time.

I glared at Chase as I caught him grinning at me once again, but I had to admit that his lighthearted attitude was refreshing. I knew that we were under dire straits, but being morose and worried all of the time was exhausting. I looked over at my dad to see that he was looking dejected and angry enough for all three of us.

Not wanting to dwell on my dad's attitude, I went back to surveying our surroundings. I knew that somewhere over our heads was heavy stone, or some other sort of barrier, but it was too dark for me to see it.

The lack of visibility was strange, considering that the city streets were lit up with various lanterns and free-floating glowing spheres. It was likely some form of illusion that obscured the ceiling with absolutes darkness. A small attempt at making an existence underground less oppressive. Although, you'd think if they were going to go to the trouble of creating an illusion, they would have made the ceiling look like a sky.

Many of the buildings that we passed looked like normal human buildings, but many were quite strange. Some were made of smooth blue or purple stone, with no seams that I could see. It was as if the stones had once been whole, and the demons simply carved out homes inside of them. Other houses were made of what looked like normal wood, but the textures of the wood grain formed elaborate shapes and swirls that accented their varying colors.

Like the houses, the roads varied between mundane and strange as well. Some stretches of the road were made from the same stone-like material as the smooth-looking houses, while other areas were cobblestone or brick. The entire city was a patchwork of different textures.

I veered to the side as a tiny man fully covered in brown fur cut between my dad and I. He wore no clothes, but the fur was shaggy enough that he wouldn't have to be censored if he was put on demon TV. If I wouldn't have moved, he would have walked straight into me.

"Demons obviously don't know their manners," I commented after the little man was out of earshot. I turned to get another look at him as he walked away, causing me to veer to the side and almost run into my dad.

"Their manners are simply different than yours," my dad commented.

I noticed that besides the small man who'd nearly run me over, many of the demons gave my dad and I a wide berth. I voiced my observations, to which he answered, "Demons know to defer to their betters."

"How are we their betters?" I asked. "We're not even pure-blooded demon." I stumbled as the road we were on switched to cobblestone.

Many of the demons that walked widely around us turned around to watch us as we went. I noticed a few looking at us from café windows, and from within alleyways as well.

My dad nodded sharply. "That might be so, but a demon's power is determined not by purity of blood, but by the bloodline itself. You and I come from a very powerful bloodline."

"And I come from the bottom of the barrel," Chase chimed in with a crooked smile.

My dad laughed. "The Naga and Necro-demon lines are very powerful in themselves," he explained for my benefit. "but the mixture of both along with human blood on both sides dilutes it a bit."

I looked to Chase for verification. He shrugged. "I'm a mutt."

My dad halted his pace in front of a building made out of golden colored bricks. The walls of the building stretched towards the ceiling and out of sight. There was no sign outside, but I could see books through one of the large windows. Apparently we had reached the library.

My father walked inside first, pausing to push his index finger into a small clear pot of black goo. Chase repeated the motion, and then gestured for me to do the same.

"What's with the pot?" I asked.

A woman in black robes with a face that closely resembled that of a lobster shushed me. Her tiny black eyes attempted to bore into me, but her strange, twitching crustacean mouth was much more intimidating than the glare. I stared at her a little too long, and she lifted her giant pincher hand and clamped her claws at the air menacingly. Chase put his arm around my shoulders and steered me forward before I ended up on the wrong side of the seafood buffet.

"What book are we looking for anyhow?" I whispered with a nervous glance back at the lobster lady.

"We're looking for a book on portals," my dad whispered. "One loophole that might help Bartimus escape the underground would be using a portal."

"What do you mean?" I prompted.

My dad began scanning the books on the shelves as he answered, "There is a barrier that prevents those of pure demon blood from passing into the human world. It has existed as long as demons have. No one knows the physics of it. Such barriers exist between many dimensions, which is why they are rarely crossed. A portal bypasses those barriers, creating an area where time and matter can flow back and forth easily."

"So why aren't all of the demons just creating portals themselves?" I asked as we walked.

"Because they can't," he answered. "It is more of a witches skill, and even then most witches would need to harness extra power to do so. It is how demons are summoned to the human world. Only the portals are not complete, and the demon can rarely fully physically manifest on the other side. As far as I know, there is only one demon who has ever been capable of creating portals without aid."

"So if *we* can't create a portal," I went on. "Then why would we research them?"

My dad sighed. "A portal is the most obvious answer to freeing a demon. Bart knows this. I believe Bart thinks that you can aid in the creation of a portal."

I scoffed. "That's insane."

My dad finally found the book he was looking for and snatched it off the shelf. "And Bart is insane. I hope it is simply his insanity that has made up the whole possibility of his escape, but we would be fools to not research all options."

I was getting seriously confused. "So now you think that we can actually get him out?"

My dad turned to walk back to the desk with the gel pot in order to check out his book. "No, but if we *can* get him out, then we can kill him and get on with our lives. If something in this book can help us, it's worth a shot."

I waited while the lobster woman ran the book over a solid square of the same black goo that was in the pot. We exited the library and I turned back to my dad. "You realize you completely contradicted yourself with that last statement, right?"

He nodded absentmindedly to me as a human-looking demon came strolling towards us and pulled him into conversation. Chase stood close to my side. His gray eyes were pinched in worry.

"What do you think?" I asked.

He jumped as if his mind had been somewhere else. He shrugged. "I don't think it's possible. Do you want some ice cream?"

I squinted up at him. "That was a strange thought jump . . . but okay?"

We walked over to a smaller sized white sphere with a cut out in the front. Another human looking demon that appeared about sixteen years old was selling ice cream cones from within the sphere. We approached the sphere and ordered, butterscotch ice cream for Chase, and green tea for me. Chase pressed his finger twice into another one of the small gel-filled pots. The gel was blue this time.

I stood there waiting, but the teenager manning the booth didn't ask for any money. Chase walked back towards my dad. I gave the kid one last glance, then jogged to catch up with Chase.

"We didn't pay," I observed as I reached him.

He smiled down at me. "The gelatum records all purchases," he explained.

"Go on," I prompted, wanting to know more about the strange system.

"The gelatum can read your DNA from the smallest touch," Chase began. "Every demon is in the network, and our purchases as well as visits to public buildings like the library are all recorded. We're billed for our purchases at the end of every month."

"And what about the visits?" I asked. "Why are those recorded?"

Chase shrugged then whispered, "The government is everywhere. Trust no one," while waggling his eyebrows at me playfully. It looked like that was all of the explanation I was going to get.

"Gee thanks Mulder," I responded sarcastically as my dad glanced over at us.

I made a mental note to ask more about the payment system later, though I'd ask my dad instead of Chase. I couldn't ask him at that moment, as the demon who'd pulled him aside was speaking excitedly about something I couldn't quite overhear. I watched my dad's conversation as I ate my ice cream and wondered what all of the excitement was about. The ice cream tasted strange, like the milk had been too near woodsmoke, and it didn't seem to melt quite like normal ice cream either.

The demon talking to my dad finally said his good-byes and walked away. My dad shifted his glance to the streets around us as we munched the last bits of our ice cream cones.

"We need to get back," he whispered. He looked around warily like someone might be watching us, making the hairs raise on my arms. "What happened?" I whispered as my dad began to hurry us along.

Chase followed behind us trying to look as normal as possible as we trotted forward. I started to notice some of the other demons giving us strange looks again. I had seen a few stares before, but I thought it was just because I was new and because of our bloodline. Now I wasn't so sure.

As we passed by an alleyway I caught sight of a small form. She looked like a little girl of around twelve or so, with long, thin black hair. The look in her eyes was not a look that a twelve year old should have. Not to mention that her pupils glowed yellow. She smiled after me as we ran past and I had to stifle a shiver.

We made our way through the streets and eventually to my dad's house. Unlike many of the other homes, the outer walls of his house were composed of cut stone and mortar. My dad opened his plain wooden front door and pushed me inside ahead of him. Chase followed.

As soon as the door was locked his worried appearance eased. Chase still looked worried though. His eyes darted around the room while he rocked back and forth on his heels with his hands in the pockets of his jeans.

My dad set about checking the windows in the large entryway, then moved on to the kitchen without a word. I turned to Chase with a questioning look. He shrugged. A lot of help he was today. I turned around and followed in the direction my dad had gone.

"What did you find out that has you so nervous?" I asked as I entered the kitchen. I didn't see my mom, Jason, or Allison anywhere, but I could hear a TV blaring in another room.

My dad looked up from where he was crouched inspecting the contents of one of the kitchen cabinets. "It is as I suspected. You are in fact the key," he explained. "At least in Bart's mind . . . and now you are the key in the mind of many others as well."

I sat down at a stool in the corner. There was no dining table anywhere in sight, only a few stools scattered about. Chase came into the kitchen followed by Jason. Both stood off to the side, not wanting to interrupt the conversation.

"What does this mean for us?" I prompted. "Does it change our plans?"

My dad shook his head quickly and stood to paw through the contents of another cabinet. "Our plans remain the same, only you are much more of a target now than I had anticipated."

"Well I'm used to being a target," I said, frustrated. When he didn't acknowledge me and instead continued shuffling things around in the cabinet, I shouted, "What the heck are you looking for!"

He finally gave up on his search and turned to face me. "Where is the ring I gave you?"

Uncomfortable, I turned my gaze down to the dark colored tiles of the floor. My dad had given me a ring that was supposedly a family heirloom. I was supposed to wear it at all times, and did originally. I had taken it off only the day before.

The ring was set with a fire-colored stone surrounded by vines. Sometimes the colors in the ring would flash and swirl, and the vines seemed to move, ever so slightly. It was creepy, to say the least. After my encounter with Bart, I had needed a break from creepy, so I stopped wearing the ring. Not that it did any good.

My dad sighed. "Where is it?" he asked impatiently.

I looked up and met his irritated gaze. "It was in my purse, which I'm assuming was left at my house."

"It's here actually," Jason chimed in. "Allison packed all of your things while we waited for the reinforcements Abel sent to arrive in Shelby."

I raised an eyebrow. "She did my laundry?" I asked, surprised. Allison wasn't the cleaning or laundry doing type.

Jason smiled. "No, your mom did that."

My dad began tapping his loafer covered foot on the tiles. I hopped off my stool and followed Jason to wherever my belongings might be. Chase remained in the kitchen with my dad.

I was led into another bedroom that I hadn't seen before. The room was barren except for a small bed, and a table covered in different vials and pouches of herbs. I had a sneaking suspicion that the bed had only been placed there for our visit, as the room seemed more like a mini alchemy lab than a bedroom. By the foot of the out-of-place bed were both mine and Allison's luggage, as well as my purse and a few of my books.

I rifled through my purse to find the ring while Jason came to crouch beside me. He reached out and pushed a strand of my hair behind my ear. "What happened while you were away?" he asked, concerned.

I found the ring, but didn't put it on my finger. "We found the book that my dad was looking for, and I nearly had an altercation with a giant lobster," I answered.

We both stood. Jason looked confused. "I'm going to ignore the giant lobster part for now," he replied. "What I meant to ask, was what happened to make your father so nervous? I can feel his energy like ants on my skin."

I shook my head. "Someone told him something, I guess. All I know is that some of the other demons know what we're doing, and they know that Bart for some reason thinks only I can make all of his dreams come true."

Jason frowned. "And now the other demons want their dreams to come true as well?"

I nodded and went for the door, not wanting to keep

my dad waiting. Jason grabbed my arm to stop me. "Wait Xoe. Why does Bartimus think that only you can free him?"

I turned my attention back to Jason. "I have no idea," I answered. "All we know is that he has never attempted something like this until now. He's gone to great lengths to dig his claws into me. Why wouldn't he have tried to rope some other half-demon, or even a full-demon for that matter, into the job?"

Jason's eyes pinched in worry. "This is all my fault," he said softly.

I pulled him into a hug. "How on earth is this your fault?" I asked.

Jason pulled away and held me at arm's length. "You encountered Bartimus because of Maggie, and you encountered Maggie because of me. If I'd been better at protecting you-"

"It would have happened anyway," I cut him off. "Bart only worked with Maggie because he already knew that he wanted me. He already had my blood before that. Maggie would have never been allowed to kill me. She was only a pawn, just like Nick."

Jason let his arms drop. "How do you know that for sure?"

I sighed. "Bart pretty much confirmed it, not verbally, but I could just tell. The whole Nick incident was Bart's fault. Bart orchestrated a whole string of murders just to get some of my blood."

"So why did Bart even need Maggie?" he questioned

as if he didn't fully believe me.

"She simply presented him with an opportunity," I explained. "He couldn't just snatch me and force me to make a deal or else. Demons have a code of conduct. It's a very loose and convoluted code, but still a code none-the-less. Saving me from Maggie created the circumstances for me to want to make a deal."

Jason grabbed my right hand and looked down at the ring, which I had slid half-way up my index finger. "And what does this have to do with anything?"

I shook my head and pulled my hand back. "Let's go find out."

Jason nodded, but was obviously reluctant when he followed me back to the kitchen. My mom was still nowhere to be seen, but Allison was now sitting on a stool beside Chase.

"Did you find it?" my dad asked as soon as Jason and I entered the room. He was leaning against the kitchen counter, attempting to act casual, but there was a strain around his eyes that gave his unease away. Perhaps the ring was more important than I'd originally been led to believe.

I walked over to him and tried to hand him the ring, but he shook his head and gestured for me to put it on. I sighed, then slowly slipped the ring back onto my index finger. I held my breath, waiting for the eerie flashing lights, but nothing happened. The ring felt like normal heavy metal on my finger.

My dad glanced at the rest of the people in the room.

"I'd like a moment alone with my daughter," he announced.

No one questioned him, though Jason looked to me for reassurance as he left the room. I gave him a nod, even though I didn't particularly feel like being alone with my father.

When everyone was gone, my dad cleared his throat to get my attention. "That ring was my mother's," he said, voice void of emotion.

I'd never heard him talk about his parents before. I knew my dad was old, at least a few centuries, maybe more. He also never spoke about his age. It had never really occurred to me that one or both of his parents might still be alive. However, they were demons, so they might be.

Full-blooded demons would basically live until someone killed them, usually another demon. Half-demons were a toss up. Some were mortal, some weren't. We didn't know yet about Chase and I. With my dad's powerful bloodline, I had a good chance at immortality, but my mom being fully human pulled those odds down. Chase had demon blood from both parents, but the lines were muddled and not quite as strong to begin with. I'd been told that he was less likely to be immortal than me, but only slightly.

"My mother used to say that the ring spoke to her," he went on, "that it showed her visions. I know you have a minor gift with premonition."

I shook my head. "I had a few dreams, that was it."

45

My dad sighed and pushed his blond hair back from his face. "Dreams of events that would soon come to pass," he corrected. "My mother started out in much the same way. She acquired the ring when she was still quite young, and was unsure if her gifts grew on their own, or because of the ring. I told you that there was only one demon that I know of that could create portals. That demon was my mother."

I blinked dumbly as I processed the information. If we could find her . . . but still, I didn't want anything to increase my powers. I quickly slipped the ring off my finger.

My dad tsked at me. "Put that back on this instant."

I placed the ring on the counter, and shook the feel of it off of my hands. "I do *not* want to cultivate psychic powers," I stated adamantly. "The future looks grim enough without me knowing exactly what will happen."

My dad snatched up the ring and held it out to me. I matched him glare for glare, and put my hands on my hips. I'd never wanted demon powers to begin with. I wasn't about to add to what I already had.

My dad lowered his hand with the ring, but continued to glare. A chiming sound went off, interrupting our glaring contest. My glare transformed to a look of question.

"Doorbell," he explained. He seemed to think for a moment, then said, "You wait here."

I followed him as he left the kitchen. Nobody puts Baby in a corner.

4

Chase was already answering the door as we reached it. A girl of about twenty-two, Chase's age, stood on the small front porch. She had long, curly red hair nearly reaching her waist, and one of those super fair complexions that would normally have freckles, but didn't. Her eyes were a similar green to mine and my fathers. She was dressed casually in jeans, a dark brown tee-shirt, and a hunter green jacket.

Once the door was all the way open, she threw herself into Chase's arms and kissed him ferociously. She had to be on the very edge of her toes to do so, as she was nowhere near Chase's 6'. The girl lowered herself to the ground and turned her gaze to me, making me realize that I'd been staring.

"You must be Xoe," she said with a smile on her flushed lips as she held her hand out to me.

I shook it briefly. Her hands were much smaller than

mine. She was almost as petite as Lucy. "And you are?" I asked, trying my best to sound friendly, but probably failing.

"I'm Josie," she said as she turned an exasperated glance up to Chase. "Apparently my *boyfriend* has told you nothing about me."

I started to sweat. Maybe another demon hot-flash was coming on. I swallowed past the lump in my throat.

"Things have been a little hectic," I said hoarsely. "I'm sure he would have if he'd had the time." I wanted to add, "Or, if it was actually important," but I didn't. Bully for me.

Chase was shifting his weight from foot to foot nervously, looking as if he wanted to end our conversation, but not knowing how.

Josie turned her attention to my dad, who had been standing silently beside me, looking mildly irritated. "You should have told me your daughter was coming, Alexondre," she chided. "I would have come over to meet her sooner."

"It was unplanned," he replied curtly, just as I said, "I just got here."

My dad offered a tight-lipped smile. "If you'll excuse us Josie, my daughter and I were in the middle of something *important*. The catching up will have to wait until a more convenient time."

I tried my very best not to smile, but on the inside I was quite pleased that my dad had been rude where I had failed. Maybe cattiness was hereditary.

"Of course," Josie answered, practically beaming with good cheer.

My dad grabbed my arm and hauled me back to the kitchen. I turned to catch a final glimpse of Josie smiling up at Chase. My stomach did a little nervous flip as I was pulled into the kitchen, obscuring the pair from my view.

"Back to the ring," my dad said, turning my attention to him. He squinted his eyes at me in concern. "Are you unwell?"

I moved my tongue around in an attempt to get some saliva in my mouth. "Um . . . yes," I answered. "I should lie down."

"We need to talk about this, Alexondra," he chided, taking naturally to the role of stern parent even though he'd been absent for most of my life.

I lifted a hand to the side of my head. "Feeling kind of dizzy over here," I lied.

My dad might have had the role of stern parent down, but I'd been faking sick my entire life. I was a seasoned pro.

My dad approached me and put a hand on the side of my neck. "You do feel a little warm," he conceded, then with a sigh added, "We'll finish this conversation later. Try not to set anything on fire."

My dad was right to be concerned, as often my previous hot flashes had ended with me burning someone or something. I didn't feel like that was going to happen this time though. In fact, I was feeling anything but angry. Tired, sick, and anxious yes, but not angry.

I numbly walked back to the bedroom that I assumed was mine, as it was the one I'd woken up in. I strained to hear some conversation from Chase and Josie, but it seemed like they'd either gone elsewhere in the house, or were outside. Or they were in the middle of a passionate make-out session. Yeah, I needed to lie down.

I went into my room and sat on the bed, but I felt too anxious to rest. I heard what sounded like a TV one room over and decided to check it out, hoping to whatever force I should pray to that Chase and Josie hadn't gone in there.

I made it to the doorway and let out a sigh of relief. Allison was watching some sort of reality show in a small den-type room. She was sprawled out on a black, over-stuffed couch that faced a gigantic TV. There were matching chairs on either side of the couch, and a large, unlit fireplace in the far wall.

"Where are mom and Jason?" I asked as I sat down on one of the chairs.

Allison rolled her eyes at me and picked imaginary lint off the sleeve of her black sweater. "Am I not good enough for you?" she asked sarcastically, or maybe not so sarcastically. With Allison, it was always kind of hard to tell.

I stood and shoved her long legs aside so I could sit on the couch next to her. She sat up with a huff of mock anger. "Your mom is resting," she explained. "I don't know where Jason is. No one will let me go anywhere, and your dad kicked us out of the kitchen, so I've just been sitting here and waiting for something to happen that I'm actually allowed to be involved in. Where's Chase?"

I suddenly felt sick again. "He's with his girlfriend," I said, trying to make the statement sound as casual as possible.

"His girlfriend!" Allison exclaimed. At my cringe, she lowered her voice and asked, "Since when does he have a girlfriend."

I shrugged and turned my gaze to the TV. "Since always, apparently. He just didn't bother to tell any of us about her."

"I find this very odd," Allison replied, turning her attention to the TV as well.

I cast a quick glance at her. I tried to not say anything for a while, but finally had to ask, "Why is it odd? I mean, he's not exactly a chatty Cathy about his past, or any of his other personal business. It's not all that unusual for him to have not told us about his girlfriend."

In reply, Allison just smiled at me, shook her head, then turned back to the TV. I opened my mouth to say more, but Chase entered the room. I waited for Josie to walk in after him, but she was nowhere to be seen. He sat on the chair that I'd originally sat on, and turned his attention to the TV as well.

I looked over at him. He sat rigidly in what was actually a rather comfy chair, his gray eyes glued firmly to the screen. As I watched him he glanced over at me, and I had to whip my eyes forward in a futile attempt to hide my staring.

Allison looked my way with another indulgent smile. "I'm going to go get something to drink," she announced. Before I could stop her, she was up and walking out of the room while I stared after her dumbfounded.

Chase and I both turned our attention back to the TV yet again. A girl was being interviewed on the screen, but she seemed rather drunk and incapable of forming words. I wasn't sure what the point of interviewing someone who could hardly speak was, but apparently her words were somehow important to the show. I pretended my best to be interested in what the girl was saying.

I watched in my peripheral vision as Chase glanced over at me again. "Sorry about that," he mumbled.

"Sorry about what?" I asked non-chalantly, keeping my eyes forward.

I saw Chase shrug out of the corner of my eye. "I haven't seen Josie in over six months. I didn't expect her to show up here as soon as we arrived. I didn't expect her to show up here at all."

I snorted and finally turned towards Chase. "Well you must not be a very good boyfriend if you haven't seen her in six months. If I were her, I would have skipped the kissing and gone straight to the punching."

Chase cringed. "We broke up . . . or at least I thought we did. I assumed her telling me that I had no ambition, and that she simply couldn't tolerate it any longer, meant that the relationship was over."

I nodded my head, feeling a strange mixture of emotions. Part of me wanted to smack Josie for being so rude, while a dark, evil part of me got some sort of satisfaction out of it. Rather than voicing any of this, I replied, "Well you don't owe me an explanation regardless."

Chase was silent for a moment, then took a deep breath as if to say more, but Jason and Allison entered the room. Jason sat down and put his arm around me. I knew he could probably sense the tension in the room, but he seemed to be ignoring it.

Chase looked at Jason and I, then looked back to the TV as he said softly, "Yeah I guess I don't."

Not paying any mind to Chase's comment, Jason looked towards me and said, "Your father has asked me to covertly convince you to wear the ring he gave you, so I ask that you please do it so that he doesn't have to be mad at me instead of you."

I laughed. "You missed your calling. You really should have been a spy."

Jason raised an eyebrow at me. "Who says I'm not?" he asked dramatically.

"Speaking of covert information," Allison began loudly. "I hear Chase has been hiding a girlfriend from us."

Chase blushed and let his dark hair fall forward to partially cover his face. "I wasn't hiding anything," he muttered in defense.

"Girlfriend?" Jason asked curiously.

Allison turned her attention towards Jason. "Yep. She just showed up at the front door. Though I only know what Xoe told me."

It was my turn to blush. I suddenly wished I had left Allison in Shelby to run around with werewolves . . . even if she would have been kidnapped by half-demons. Neither beastie would have stood a chance against her.

I could feel everyone's eyes on me as I looked down at my lap. I turned to glare at Allison. "You asked where Chase was," I stated bluntly. "And I told you."

"Xoe," Jason began hesitantly. "Can I speak with you?"

I nodded, feeling like a child that had just been caught cheating in school. Jason and I stood. I turned another glare at Allison as we walked out of the room. Jason went past my room and back towards the room with my belongings where we'd gone to fetch the ring, leaving me no choice but to follow. We sat down together on the bed, and I waited for him to speak.

Jason grabbed my hand, then used his free hand to turn my chin up towards him. "Is there something between you and Chase?" he asked simply, causing my heart to stop.

My jaw dropped. "A-absolutely not," I stammered. It was the truth. Sure, I had come to the conclusion that I felt some confusing feelings in regards to Chase, but nothing more than that.

Jason smiled hesitantly. "I had to ask. I've just noticed . . . " he trailed off.

"Noticed what?" I prompted, not actually wanting him to continue, but not wanting to seem guilty either. Really, I had nothing to feel guilty over. Now if only the angry butterflies in my stomach would agree with me.

"Just," he paused as if searching for the right words. "Like just now with Allison," he went on. "She called him out for hiding his girlfriend and made it seem . . . " he hesitated again. "She made it seem like maybe he has feelings for you, or maybe you didn't like hearing the news about him having a girlfriend."

"I can't speak for his feelings," I admitted, "but I can assure you that nothing is going on between us."

Jason nodded. "But you think he has feelings for you then?" he prompted.

I shrugged. "I told you I can't speak for his feelings. If he has any, he's never expressed them to me."

"But do you *think* he has them?" he pressed again.

"Why are you pushing this?" I snapped. "I'm not Chase. If you want to know his feelings, ask him yourself."

Jason cringed. "I'm sorry. I just-" he paused, "all I need to know is that you don't have feelings for him."

"Well I don't," I replied hotly.

Jason watched me for a moment, then said, "Well I must say, I am relieved."

I let out my breath, feeling a certain measure of relief myself, and also feeling silly that the whole conversation had to take place to begin with. I had no place being territorial about Chase. He was my friend, and had the right to date whomever he wanted. Even if she was overly-confident and rude.

Jason pulled me close to him, and we snuggled up in silence for a while. I could still hear the TV two rooms away, and somewhere in the house my dad was clattering through cabinets again, but our room was at least silent.

I'd lied when I'd spoken about Chase's feelings for me. I was pretty sure that he did in fact have them. I might have had a few feelings myself, and it was making my head spin more than anything else that was going on. While I was unsure about my feelings for Chase, I knew for a fact that I loved Jason, and shouldn't have been thinking about Chase or his pretty little girlfriend at all.

On that train of thought, I also made a promise to myself to not be jealous of Josie. Just because I had a bad first impression of her, didn't mean I actually knew anything about her or her relationship with Chase.

What it all came down to was that Josie was none of my business. I had enough business of my own to attend to anyhow. Of course, the hardest part of any type of business is minding your own.

5

While we were busy with our dramatic issues of the heart, or what-have-you, my dad had concocted a plan. Kind of. Jason and I were still sitting on the bed when he'd found us. He made a beeline for the alchemy table as soon as he entered the room. Jason and I rose and looked over his shoulders while he deftly began mixing herbs and powders together.

The thing he had been looking for in all of the kitchen cabinets was a recipe book, and not the kind for food either. The book that he scanned with his fingertips as he measured out different substances looked ancient, and was written in a language I had never seen before.

He threw the last pinch of powder into the large metal pot, then turned to me. "Fire please."

"Why can't you do it?" I asked, feeling crabby.

My dad sighed. "It's good practice."

"I've had enough practice," I groaned.

My dad huffed. "Humor me."

I took a deep breath and rolled my shoulders a few times to relieve some tension. With how on edge I was, making a fire should have been easy, but I was just too distracted. I forced my brain to be silent and walked through the visualization I always did in my head before using my powers. The visualization was finally starting to become second nature to me, and didn't take nearly as long as it had in the beginning. As I opened my eyes, a flame flashed into existence in the pot.

Without a word of thanks my dad stirred the contents of the pot with a long metal spoon. Next he grabbed a large vial of dark liquid and poured it into the pot, extinguishing the flame I'd just created. He stirred the contents again, then used a small metal funnel to pour the resulting liquid into a clean glass vial.

He stood and handed the vial to me with pride. "You'll need to drink this before bed tonight. Every last drop, and no spitting it out," he warned.

I took the tiny vial and examined its contents, not liking the idea that he thought I'd want to spit it out. "I don't think I'll be thirsty," I decided, then asked, "What's it supposed to do?"

My dad smiled proudly. "It's to help you to dream. You're going to find my mother."

"Like heck I am!" I exclaimed. "I told you I don't want to have any more prophetic dreams. They're always about bad things, and we *so* have enough bad things to deal with already."

"This won't be a prophetic dream," he assured. "It's more of a . . . tracking dream. You'll be able to travel between realms, not physically of course. Think of it like astral projection. Your body will remain here, while a part of you searches the other planes. You will use the ring to find her. Rings like that always want to return to their owners."

"This seems dangerous," Jason said as he pulled me close to him, "and it could ultimately be fruitless."

My dad ignored him, and spoke to me instead. "It's not dangerous. You will only be there mentally. When you wake up, you'll still be safe in your bed. Nothing can harm you as long as we have your body."

"Why can't *you* do it?" I asked. "I've never even met your mother. She won't know who I am."

"I don't have any talent in premonition or dream-walking. The two go hand in hand. If you can do one, you should be able to do the other," he answered.

"She still won't know who I am," I pressed.

My dad rolled his eyes. "You're well aware that we have a strong family resemblance. I'm quite sure that she'll recognize you for who you are. Appearance-wise, you could easily pass for her sister."

"Except slightly younger, of course," I countered.

My dad's face gave away the fact that he was beginning to lose patience with me. It was a look that I'd become accustomed to. "Most immortals stop aging at some point. Some take longer than others, but your grandmother looks the same age as I do."

Considering that my dad looked around 35, and a well-maintained 35, I really probably could pass for my grandmother's sister. The thought was unnerving, to say the least. It would be strange to have a family photo together . . . not that such a thing was likely to happen.

"And what am I supposed to do with my grandmother when I find her?" I asked weakly. "She's obviously not terribly concerned with our lives. Why would she even help us?"

"She will help us simply to keep her line from dying out," he replied. "She has no interest in my life, because she has been assured that my continued survival is not an issue. So, you will find her and ask her to teach you how to create a portal. If you can create a portal, we can free Bart. Him being out of his lair and in the human world will level the playing field. It would take him time to learn how to use his powers in the new environment. We would be able to defeat him."

My knees felt weak. I sat down in my dad's vacated chair and looked up at him. "Say this all works, and I'm somehow able to make a portal. Bart has to know that we don't want him running free, which means he'll be expecting an attack. He'll have a plan."

"But he does not know the difference between magic here, and magic in the human world," my dad countered. "It takes time to develop the same skills in the human world that come so easily to us underground."

"Fine," I answered, out of arguments. If dream-walking was as safe as he claimed, we had nothing to lose in trying. Plus I had to admit, the prospect of meeting my demon grandmother was more than a little intriguing.

"It is not fine," Jason argued. "This whole plan is insane."

My dad and I both looked at him like he was being silly. Jason scoffed. "And if you figure out how to open portals, what then?" he asked. "The other demons are foaming at the mouth just at the possibility."

"They won't need to know," my dad replied. "As soon as Bart is free, I'll kill him. There will be no one else to speak of portal making. In fact, without Bart's gossip spurring other demons into action, they will move on with their lives and find other things to focus upon."

"Plus," I added, "if I can make portals, then I'll easily be able to escape any demons that try to get their hands on me."

My dad nodded his agreement excitedly.

Jason's mouth hung open, but he didn't offer any further argument. It seemed things were settled. There was a moment of silence, then my stomach spoke up. The ice cream hadn't been terribly filling, and I was running on empty.

I turned back to my dad. "How does one acquire dinner in the demon underworld?" I asked.

My dad smiled. "One orders out." He turned on his heel and left the room, presumably to place a food order.

"I don't like this Xoe," Jason said as soon as my father had left.

"I'll tell you what," I soothed. I rubbed my hands up and down his arms in an attempt to ease his nerves. "You can stay next to me while I sleep. If it seems like I'm panicking or something isn't going right, you can just wake me up."

"And what if you don't wake up?" he countered.

"Then my dad will know what to do," I assured, though I wasn't actually entirely sure of that fact.

Jason nodded, but he obviously still wasn't happy with the situation. He seemed like he was about to say more, but then he turned his head as if listening to something in the distance. "Someone is here," he noted.

He had probably heard the front door. Vampire hearing is creepy. "Are you sure it wasn't my dad leaving to get food?"

Jason shook his head. "I can hear him talking to your mother."

I found myself wondering how many of my conversations Jason had overheard over the time we'd been together. The thought upped the creepy factor of his supernatural hearing more than a little.

"Let's go see," I said, needing to do something other than stand there.

Jason followed me out of the room, through the kitchen, and to the front door. Allison had answered it, which she wasn't supposed to do. We were trying to keep it on the down-low that we had brought a human and a vampire to the underground, and having the human answer the front door was a tad counterproductive.

Standing outside of the doorway trying to talk their way in were Josie and another demon. At least, I assumed he was a demon since he was walking around freely in the demon underground. I glared around Allison's back at Josie's smiling face. Maybe no one should have answered the door at all.

Josie was now dressed in tight-fitting jeans and a long-sleeve shirt with horizontal black and white stripes. I wasn't sure why she'd changed when she'd only been gone for a short while. I had to admit that the new outfit was slightly more becoming than the last. Maybe she wanted to impress Chase.

The boy beside her was about Max's height, which was pretty short. He looked vaguely like Josie, only with light brown hair instead of red, and pale blue eyes instead of green. He wore all black, and it suited his demeanor. He didn't look terribly interested in the conversation that Allison and Josie were having.

Allison turned to me and Jason when she realized we had entered the room. "They say they're here to see Chase . . . again. Were we expecting any visitors?" What she meant was, do I have permission to be completely catty to this girl, simply based on the fact that she's dating Chase, and we don't like new people, because we don't like change?

I rubbed at a spot of tension between my eyes. "Hi

Josie," I said begrudgingly. "I'll get Chase for you." Then I walked away.

I really wasn't trying to be rude. Okay, I wasn't trying to be *that* rude. I honestly didn't know if my dad wanted extra visitors. We were after-all trying to keep everything we were doing a secret. Inviting guests along for the ride didn't seem like the best way to do that.

Jason waited with Allison and the visitors while I went in search of Chase. I checked a few empty rooms before I finally found him lying on a bed in a room at the very end of the hall.

Many of the rooms in my dad's house were non-descript, and probably didn't even serve as bedrooms on a day-to-day basis. This one was different. It was very . . . lived in. It seemed that Chase had been given a room in my dad's house quite a while ago. It made sense I suppose. I knew he didn't have a house or apartment of his own, even though he's twenty-two.

The room didn't have much in the way of décor, but there was a sturdy wooden desk with books strewn about, as well as a dresser with several drawers left open. Unfolded clothes peeked out of the drawers, begging to be ironed.

Chase was lying on his back, staring at the ceiling. He turned his head to look at me as I stood awkwardly in the doorway. "You can come in," he said apathetically.

I stepped into the room at his invitation, but didn't go any farther. "Josie and another demon are at the door. I'm not sure if my dad wants people over, so . . ."

Chase looked back up at the ceiling. "It's probably her brother, Verril," he commented, but didn't get up. His slight accent made the name Verril sound strange. I was so used to hearing Chase speak that I didn't think about his accent much. He'd never told me where he was born or how he acquired it. He never really told me anything about his past period.

I sighed. "Well they're your . . . friends. So you should probably come and see to them and convince them that we don't have a human and a vampire staying down here with us, even though the human in question answered the door."

Chase rolled out of bed and walked right past me. Not even so much as a thank you. I hesitated for a moment, then stomped after him. I briefly considered throwing a fireball at his back, then decided not to be petty.

"It's none of your business what I am," I heard Allison say as I neared the room. Crap, they were figuring it out. Demons don't have a supernatural sense of smell like werewolves, so we can't instantly tell what type of supernatural a person is right away. We can, on the other hand, somewhat sense when someone isn't a demon.

"There you are," Josie said as her attention turned from Allison to Chase. Jason was standing back in the corner, far enough to stay out of the argument, but close enough to protect Allison if she needed it.

Chase glanced at me before he walked over to Josie. "I told you it's not really a good time," he told her. "I have a lot of things to do for Alexondre."

Josie rolled her eyes. "Let me handle Alexondre. I've missed you. I won't take no for an answer."

She pushed her way past Allison and walked into the house. I gave Chase a *you deal with it* look, grabbed Allison, and went into the kitchen with Jason bringing up the rear.

"What on earth is going on in there?" My dad asked as we appeared. He had a phone cradled against his cheek, and dozens of take-out menus in his hands.

Josie barged into the kitchen behind us. "Just order pizza," she said. "It's the easiest thing with all of these *random* people around here."

"Speaking of *random* people," I began, but stopped at a glare from Chase as he entered the kitchen as well.

Verril walked in behind Chase and went to lean silently against the far wall. Apparently we were having a party. Fun fun.

"Josie, this isn't the best time," my dad said slowly as he tried very hard to keep his expression friendly.

"I haven't been around in *months*," she whined. "And it seems like no one is even happy to see me."

I was liking her less and less. I had the urge to tell her that she was right, and that no one was happy to see her, but held my tongue. I'd been doing that a lot lately, and it rankled.

My dad took a deep breath. I was pretty sure he was counting to ten. "Pizza it is," he said finally. He handed the phone to Chase. He looked around for a moment more, then announced, "I'm going to go check on Libby."

I watched my dad leave. He was the last person my mom would want checking on her, but voicing my opinion would do no good now. It was probably a lie anyhow, since Jason had heard them talking when he had *actually* gone to check on her a few minutes before.

Chase dialed a number into the phone without looking at any of the takeout menus, and waited while it rang. Apparently he knew the number for pizza by heart. As Chase ordered, I wondered if our delivery guy or gal would look like a human, or if we'd receive our pizza from another giant lobster or some other form of fish-person. Would they be offended if we ordered anchovies?

Josie entwined her arm with Chase's and hung off of him while he placed the order. She looked like a teenage girl enamored with her first crush. I seriously hoped I didn't look like that when I was around Jason.

"Thirty minutes," Chase announced as he hung up the phone. He appeared more than a little uncomfortable with Josie being at his side, but he didn't pull away from her either. He caught me watching them and stared back at me defiantly. I glared right back. Glaring contests are kind of my thing.

Since there was no dining room table, Josie and Verril began pulling stools up to the large kitchen counter. The rest of us watched them silently. Personally I was considering just taking a few slices of pizza to eat in my room.

"I've told your dad a million times to buy a proper table," Josie said looking at me. "I used to eat dinner over here almost every night . . . well the nights when Chase wasn't out watching over you-"

I was pretty sure she had hoped to surprise me with the information that Chase had been watching me from afar long before we met, but she failed on that point. Chase had already told me. It wasn't anything weird.

Sometimes when my dad wasn't available to check on me, he would send Chase in his stead. I suspected that Josie had not been a fan of Chase filling in, even if he was just following orders. Heck, I might be a little salty too if I'd had to deal with Jason checking in on another girl all of the time. Although, I would probably take it out on the guy instead of the unsuspecting girl.

I snorted, "Sorry for stealing him away so much," I replied sarcastically. I didn't care if I was being rude. She'd started it.

Jason grabbed my hand, a reminder to not let my temper get too out of control. I couldn't burn other demons, but I could easily destroy my dad's kitchen by setting things on fire around her.

Allison sat down on one of the stools that Verril had moved, then grinned over at me, obviously enjoying the whole scene. Josie slammed the next stool down with more force than was necessary, then sat and spun on her stool to face me. "So I hear you're quite popular among werewolves," she prompted. "A real alpha queen, or would that be alpha bi-"

"Josie!" Chase snapped, cutting her off mid-word.

I glared at Chase, who had obviously been blabbing

since Josie had first come a'callin, but he raised his hands in an *I didn't do it* gesture. I turned back to Josie. "Says who?" I asked calmly.

Josie shrugged. "Word gets around. It's not every day a demon decides to sully herself by hanging out with dogs." She started to spin around on her stool as if very bored with our conversation.

My first thought was that Josie was *so* lucky that Lucy wasn't with us, because that smug smile would have been wiped clean by now. My second thought was that I didn't like the fact that Josie had kept tabs on me. Sure word gets around, but she wouldn't have made note of it if she weren't intentionally trying to find out about me. I was about to ask again *exactly* how she had heard about my interactions with werewolves, but the doorbell rang.

"That was fast," Verril commented as he glanced at the clock on the wall. It was the first time I'd heard him speak. His voice was calculated and confident, and not really what I had expected from the quiet guy sitting in the corner.

Instead of turning to Chase, Josie looked up at Jason. "Be a dear and help me get the pizzas?"

Jason shifted from foot to foot, but finally nodded. He gave my hand a squeeze, then followed Josie out of the kitchen. I stared after Jason and wished that I'd interjected.

"That was seriously like only five minutes," I grumbled. "Demon pizza services sure are a lot faster than human ones."

Chase seemed confused. He looked over to Verril, who shrugged, then said, "It could have been her."

Perplexed, I looked back to Chase for an explanation. Before he could say anything, there was a crash somewhere near the front door, and then a thud. I started toward the room and ended up converging with Chase in the doorway as we both rushed forward.

Josie stood over Jason with a knife in her hand. He was on the ground, not moving. I was too stunned to act. Blood slowly pooled around Jason's prostrate form.

"W-why?" Chase whispered, obviously in shock as well.

Josie twirled the knife in her hand and turned towards me. "You shouldn't have gone where Bartimus couldn't reach you," she said with a smile. "He didn't like it. He figured you were trying to find a way out of your deal."

The blood continued to pool around Jason. He was a vampire. A knife shouldn't be able to kill him so easily, but tell that to the feeling of dread clouding my mind.

I walked purposefully towards Josie. All of my fear and other thoughts were drowned out in a high-pitched hum of rage. I wasn't sure what I'd do when I reached her, but I damn well didn't need demon powers in order to kill her.

She brandished the knife at me. "He's not dead," she said quickly, a hint of nerves tainting her bravado. "At least not yet," she continued as she took a step back and pointed the knife at me. "The blade is coated in a certain type of poison, but I won't tell you which. Bart knows, and can save him . . . once you deliver what you promised," she finished quickly.

I lunged for Josie, not caring about the knife. Surprisingly, she withdrew it and hopped to the side to narrowly avoid my rush. She calmly snapped her fingers and her form went transparent like a hologram. "Tick tock, Xoe. Tick tock," she said, then disappeared entirely.

No longer having anything to attack, I rushed to Jason's side. I gently rolled him over on his back. His chest moved as he breathed, but just barely. His blood soaked into the knees of my jeans. It had already grown cool from its time spent on the floor.

Chase hesitated at my side as Verril and Allison came into view in the doorway to the kitchen. I looked at Verril and found myself barely able to speak. I summoned a fireball in the palm of my hand, not caring whether or not it could hurt him. I couldn't set a demon on fire, or burn one, but maybe I could throw fire *at* one. I was about to test the theory.

He held up his hands to ward off the blow. "I didn't know!" he shouted right as I threw it.

My dad came rushing into the room and intercepted the fireball right before it hit Verril. It paused a few inches from my dad's chest, and then winked out into nothing. "What is-" he began, then his eyes went down to Jason.

"What happened?" he ordered.

The tears finally began streaming down my face as I crouched back down beside Jason. I tried to grip his loose hand, but it was covered with blood and slipped back to the floor. Chase quickly explained to my dad what had happened.

My dad came to my side and tore Jason's shirt open over the wound. He lifted his hand up and a thick wad of gauze appeared in his palm. He pressed it to Jason's stomach in an attempt to stop the blood flow.

"The knife was poisoned," I explained quickly.

"Even with poison, his wound should be healing," he said worriedly. "He should not still be bleeding."

"What do we do?" I asked as I wiped the tears off my face, forgetting about the blood on my hands. All of my own blood was rushing to my head, threatening to make me pass out.

My dad gave me a concerned look, then turned to Chase. Allison was huddled in the corner of the room, trying to not get in the way. "Help me lift him," my dad said to Chase as he secured the gauze to Jason's stomach with some medical tape he'd manifested.

"Oh my!" a cry sounded from the side of the room. My mom had finally emerged at the worst possible time. Her face went white, but I didn't have it in me to comfort her.

My dad lifted Jason under his shoulders while Chase took a hold of his feet. "To the back bedroom," my dad instructed, referring to the room with his alchemy table in it.

They started carrying him away, my alarmingly life-less vampire. Josie had said he wouldn't die yet, and that Bart could cure him. Somehow I didn't believe it. It was up to us to cure him . . . if we could.

My mom clutched at my arm as I followed the procession to the back bedroom. "You're covered in blood," she said softly.

I nodded. "I know," I said, then kept walking.

As I left the room I saw Allison go to my mom and pull her into a hug. I was grateful to have Allison there to take care of her. At that moment I couldn't focus on anything but Jason.

I entered the bedroom as my dad and Chase were lying Jason down gently on the bed. Chase stood back as my dad set to checking Jason's vital signs, and repacking his bandage.

Chase came to stand beside me. "Xoe-" he began.

"No," I interrupted. "This is your fault. *You* let her in here."

Chase looked hurt, and I didn't care. Maybe he didn't deserve all of the blame, but I needed to blame someone, and he was the only one available at the moment. I looked away from Chase's hurt expression and back down at Jason. Chase and I were not going to be the only ones hurting because of this. Josie was going to pay. I'd make sure of it.

6

"You will need to find my mother tonight," my dad said after we'd made Jason as stable as possible.

"I can't!" I argued. "I can't leave him like this," I said more calmly, though the tears had started again. I looked down at Jason's perfectly still form. If I left and he . . . I shook my head slowly. I couldn't even think about it.

My dad gave me a sympathetic look. "I cannot fix this Xoe," he said. "I know nothing of poisons. We need to find out if you can open a portal. Helping Bart is our only option."

I took a deep, shaky breath. "I can't even think about portals and demons right now. We have to make him okay. Nothing else matters."

"This is the only way, Xoe," my dad said. "Perhaps if we can find your grandmother, she may even know how to help him. If not, she can help us make a portal for Bart."

Chase stood off to one side, staring down at Jason and pretending to not hear our conversation. He looked miserable. I hoped he wouldn't mind when I killed Josie. Then again, I didn't really care what he thought of it. I was doing it regardless.

While we were taking care of Jason, my dad had explained Josie's powers to me. Her main talents were in telekinesis. She had made the doorbell ring, not the pizza guy. The pizza had eventually come, but Allison or my mom had taken care of it.

Josie could also transport her body with her mind, which was how she'd escaped so quickly. The majority of demons couldn't travel like that. My dad could pop out and leave just a puff of smoke in his wake. I'd been told I could probably learn to do it, but it hadn't come to me yet.

Verril had slipped out at some point while I was focused on Jason. It was unfortunate. We could have used him as leverage against Josie. Of course, she'd left him behind to begin with, so I somehow thought that wouldn't have worked anyhow. Apparently family didn't matter much to some demons.

I glanced at Jason again. "I'll do it," I said finally.

My dad nodded. "Good. You need to eat something. You haven't eaten all day, and you will need your strength. Dream-walking can be highly draining."

I looked down at my bloody clothes. I didn't want to

leave Jason, but I would need a shower before I went to sleep in an attempt to find my grandmother. My suitcases were still in the room, so I wiped my hands clean on my jeans as much as possible and started looking through them for a new outfit. It would have made sense to just put on pajamas, but I just needed to be in more sturdy clothes at that moment.

I'd seen where the bathroom was earlier, so I just left without saying anything to my dad or Chase. I couldn't bear another look at Jason as I left. It was just too frightening seeing him that way. My instincts were screaming at me to go after Bart directly, but me dying wouldn't do Jason much good.

I walked into the bathroom and locked the door. Once I was alone, I let out a breath I hadn't realized I'd been holding. The bathroom was white and sterile looking, with pale green rugs and shower curtain. I put my clean clothes on the closed toilet lid and started the water in the shower.

Taking off my bloody jeans turned out to be quite a task as the thick, soaked fabric clung to my skin. Sadly, that wasn't even my first time taking off bloody jeans in the last week. The last time they'd been covered in Chase's blood after a vampire attack. The vampire had nearly ripped his shoulder off. I hadn't seen the wound again since it had happened, but he was likely still healing it. Chase is the slowest healer out of us all.

I finished undressing and stepped into the shower.

There was enough blood still on my skin that it turned the stream of water pink. I watched numbly as Jason's blood ran down the drain.

I scrubbed my skin and hair thoroughly, but I didn't want to get out of the shower. Once I got out I'd have to deal with Jason's situation again. I'd have to go into my dreams to find a semi-ancient demon whom I'd never met. She probably didn't even know I existed, despite my dad's assurances. My father never said why they'd lost touch, and I knew I'd probably never get it out of him. He had a bad habit of not volunteering information until it was absolutely necessary.

With a sigh I turned off the water and dried myself off. There was no postponing it any longer. Plus, my dad had said I needed to eat. I didn't feel like eating, but if it would get me one step closer to finding a cure for Jason, I'd do it. I never thought I'd see the day that I would need any extra motivation to eat pizza.

I dressed in deep gray, form-fitting jeans a dark green flannel that I'd previously stolen from Jason. I ran my fingers through my damp hair and noticed that I still had some of Jason's blood under my fingernails. More blood was going to be spilled before all of this was over. Here's hoping it wouldn't be more of ours.

I left the bathroom and made my way into the kitchen where I found Allison and my mother. My mom was taking small bites from a piece of pizza while Allison stared down at her plate with a distant expression. They had found a small table to put pizza on, and sat on stools around it.

Allison looked up at me with hollow eyes. "How is he?"

I shrugged and sat down at the table across from them. "Not good, but hopefully I'll find a way to help him tonight."

"Why did that girl attack him?" my mom asked, her voice sounding small and frail like a child.

I looked down at the mostly full box of pizza with distaste. "Because of me," I answered morosely. "It's my fault."

"It's not your-" Allison began, but I held up a hand to cut her off. Allison looked down at her plate and mumbled, "It's Chase's fault for bringing that girl here."

I didn't argue with her. I agreed, at least in part. Josie had stabbed Jason because of me, but she'd been allowed in the house in the first place because of Chase. We'd been stupid to trust her. It was just too much of a coincidence, her showing up out of the blue after they'd allegedly been apart for six months.

I looked at my mom as she stared down at her plate. This would probably be the proverbial straw, and my mom would be the proverbial camel. She had shut down after I told her what I was, and what my friends were. It had been a lot to take in. I'd managed to handle it, because it was either handle it or die. I was beginning to realize that maybe my mom wasn't quite capable of handling it like I had. That maybe she no longer wanted me around at all.

I felt tears welling up in my eyes again. Allison reached across the table and grabbed my hand. My mom just looked down at the table like her back was already broken.

7

I decided to lie and tell my dad that I had eaten. I wanted to get to sleep as soon as possible, and sitting at a table in silence with my mother and Allison wasn't furthering that cause. I eyed the potion that would allegedly help me dream-walk. Not only would it put me in a very deep sleep, but it would allow me to have control over my dream-state, or so my father had said.

The vial of liquid was on the small table beside my bed, looking harmless and unassuming. I snatched it up and examined it more closely. The liquid inside was dark and thick looking. It coated the sides of the vial as I rolled it back and forth in my palm.

"Are you going to drink that, or just mind meld with it?" Allison asked from her perch by my feet.

I gave her a dirty look, then turned my attention

thoughtfully back to the vial. Allison sat at the foot of my bed and waited. Chase was also in the room, though he kept his distance. It would be his job to wake me if it seemed like something was going wrong. It was supposed to be Jason's job. If I couldn't have him, I would have preferred that Allison did it, but I might freak out and accidentally burn her. Since Chase was a demon, him waking me was safer.

My dad could have woken me as well, but he was monitoring Jason, and keeping an eye on my mom as well. I didn't think Josie would come back, but I didn't want my mom to be unprotected just in case. It was Chase's job to look after Allison and me.

I pulled the stopper out of the vial and thought of Jason. I'd have to trust my dad to keep him alive until I got back. I let out a breath, then threw back the liquid in one shot. It tasted like bitter molasses and left a trail of cold behind as it slid down my throat. I closed my eyes and thought of what I thought my grandmother might look like. My dad had told me that it would be helpful to think of her, but it was kind of difficult since I'd never met her. Therefore I just pictured the made-up version of my grandmother that I had in my head.

"I don't feel-" I began, then a wave of nausea crashed into me. I started to move from the bed, feeling like I was going to vomit, but Chase rushed over and held me down. My stomach twisted into violent knots, causing me to convulse against Chase's hands on my shoulders.

"What's happening to her!" Allison shouted.

"I don't know!" Chase replied through gritted teeth.

I kept my thoughts focused on my grandmother, not wanting to end up in some dream that had nothing to do with her. Suddenly the pain subsided, as did the pressure Chase was putting on my shoulders. I looked up at the ceiling, which currently seemed to be dripping with black goo, then closed my eyes again. I felt a rush of movement like I was being tossed into the air. When I opened my eyes, I was at an empty bus depot.

It was sometime late at night, and the only illumination came from a lone street lamp near the wooden bench I was sitting on. I was sitting outside in front of an empty four-lane street. The depot behind me was dark and void of people. The dark glass of the depot's windows showed me my reflection clearly, and nothing else, at least at first. As I watched, something in the reflection changed.

Behind my reflection self, a large, dark shape loomed. It curled over me like a creature rearing up on its hind legs. I couldn't make out a definite figure, but the swirling shape was defined enough for me to see its two arms nearing my shoulders.

I frantically dove off of the bench and rolled across the ground, banging my elbow against the concrete as I went. I turned as quickly as I could to look at the creature, but nothing was there. Yet, when I looked back at the reflective glass, the shape was still present. It flowed towards me again, and I nearly tripped over myself getting to my feet. I kept my eyes on the reflection, rather than looking in front of me as the creature's form writhed towards me. I calmed my pulse long enough to concentrate and create a ball of flame in my palm.

The fire was an eerie pure-red in color, which made me nervous. Usually, my fire looked like normal flames. The odd color had only happened one other time. The shadow-shape reared back away from the flame. Still watching the reflection, I took a step towards the shadow, leading with my hand.

The creature let out a loud shriek and dissipated into the night. I let out a breath of relief, but didn't extinguish my fire. I took another step and looked up and down the dark street, unsure of where to go. My dad had told me the ring would lead me to his mother, but it was lifeless on my finger.

Out of nowhere a suspicious looking taxi cab came to a screeching halt on the street in front of me. I hadn't seen it approach, it was just suddenly there, causing me to jump and lose my flame. The cab looked like a normal yellow cab, but was covered in dents and rust, like it had sat on the beach for ten years. What I could see of the empty passenger seat looked like it had some sort of mold or algae on it.

The woman in the driver's seat leaned over towards the passenger's side so she could see me. She had silver-colored skin that seemed to sparkle with microscopic glitter. Her hair was long, pin-straight, and perfectly white.

The hair brushed the passenger's seat as she leaned over a little closer to roll down the window. The woman looked up at me with icy blue eyes that seemed to glitter just like her skin, then flashed me a perfect smile. "Need a ride tater-tot?" she asked in a voice like broken glass.

I cringed at the sound. "Maybe . . . " I began, not sure if getting in the cab would be a good idea.

She gave me another smile. "First timer?" she asked. Her voice raised goosebumps on my arms. "We don't see many new dreamers around here," she went on.

"Dreamers?" I asked, then instantly regretted showing my ignorance. Demons tended to take advantage of ignorance.

"Those who can walk the dreamlands to travel to different planes," she explained. "I'm Dorrie."

She held out one shimmering hand to me. I eyed it for a moment, then took it reluctantly. Her skin felt like sandpaper. I withdrew my hand too quickly in shock and ended up losing a little bit of skin off of my palm as a result.

Dorrie giggled at me. "Where are you trying to go?" she asked.

I considered lying, but I wasn't doing so well on my own, and maybe she could actually help. "I'm looking for my grandmother," I answered.

She laughed. "On your way to grannies? You better get in before any wolves find you."

The door of the cab opened on its own, and Dorrie leaned back over to her side. I looked around the bus depot nervously. More dark shapes swirled in the reflection of the glass, and I could hear a scuttling that sounded like a group of rats on the pavement.

I got into the cab without thinking and slammed the door. I half expected Dorrie to turn to me and reveal her evil plan, but she only smiled. Now that I could see her fully, I noticed that she wore a white, sleeve-less jumpsuit of sorts with a little name tag sewn onto the chest pocket.

When I didn't say anything she asked, "What realm is your grannie in?"

"I-I'm not sure," I stammered and held out my hand with the ring on it. "I'm supposed to be able to find her with this."

Dorrie took a close look at the ring. "Let me guess," she said. "Sometimes it shimmers, sometimes it doesn't?"

I nodded, wondering how she knew.

"The ring is broken pop-tart. I know a good repair guy I could take you to." She started driving down the road, presumably towards the repair guy.

"I don't have time to go to a repair guy!" I exclaimed quickly.

The cab came to a halt again, flinging me forward. Dorrie sighed. "Do you at least know your grandmother's name?"

My jaw dropped. My father had never mentioned her name.

"Your parents names?" she questioned. "You have to at least know those."

"Alexondre is my father," I answered hopefully. "It's his mother that I'm trying to find."

"What, like Cher? What's his last name dumpling?" she asked.

I was beginning to get nervous the longer we weren't moving. I could still see the bus depot in the rear-view mirror. "Demons have last names?" I asked.

Dorrie shook her head. "Their demon bloodlines have names crumpet," she explained. "Man, you're not just new to dream-walking. How did you even manage to find your way here?"

"I drank a potion-" I began.

"Let me see the ring again," she interrupted.

I held up my hand and she snatched the ring off of my finger before I could react. She held it close to her sparkling eye for a moment. Seemingly satisfied, she handed the ring back and started driving.

"Where are we going?" I asked.

"I've seen the ring before," she said, "a very long time ago. I'll take you to its previous owner, but be warned. A ring like that would have been coveted when it was still fully functional. It's probably had a lot of owners. The one we find might not be your granny."

"Will it take long to get there?" I asked with renewed anxiety.

Dorrie nodded as the cab picked up speed. "It's several realms away. Sit tight pumpkin pie."

Up ahead on the road was a giant yellow wall. It seemed to be made of some kind of semi-transparent gel, and reached up as far as my eyes could see. The headlights of the cab shone through it as we approached at full speed.

"Watch out!" I screamed right before we hit the wall.

The cab seemed to go in slow motion as it pushed its way through the gel. We came out the other side with a loud *pop*.

Dorrie did not seem ruffled in the slightest. "That was a realm crossing," she explained. "We'll be going through quite a few."

"You could have warned me," I choked out as I tried to relearn how to breathe.

"Sorry," she said. "I've been doing this for so long that I don't even think about it anymore."

"How long exactly?" I asked, still having a bit of trouble breathing.

"I don't really remember," she said. "This is what I was created for. The beginning of my time on the road was the beginning of my existence."

"Wait," I began, confused, "you do other things besides driving this cab, right?"

Dorrie shook her head. "It's what I was made for."

I stared at Dorrie. She seemed completely at peace with what she was saying. "You're not a demon?" I asked, still confused.

She smiled. "Heavens no pork chop. The demons made me. Without me, traveling between realms takes ages."

I shook my head. "They made you? I don't understand. You can't just *make* a person. Even if they could, don't you want to do anything else?"

Dorrie laughed. "I'm a golem of sorts. My insides are hollow and I'm not meant to live like others. There's nothing else for me to do." She glanced over at me. "This is what I'm made for," she repeated. "It's good to have a purpose."

We went through another wall, a pink one this time. The process made me dizzy, but I didn't react as poorly as I had the first time.

"Hollow?" I asked once we were through the crossing, getting more hung up on that idea than all of the other crazy things she was telling me.

Dorrie flipped her long white hair over her shoulder and nodded. "I have no insides. I am a construct of demon magic, so I don't need them."

I looked at her glistening skin and had the sudden urge to knock my fist on her arm and see if it sounded hollow. Don't worry, I resisted. Instead I asked, "Could you stop driving? You know, hypothetically, if you wanted to."

Dorrie seemed to think about my question for a moment. "I suppose I could," she answered. "Though I've never heard of any of the other drivers doing it. I don't see any reason why I would stop."

"There are more of you?" I asked.

She nodded. "I've never seen them, but my passengers have mentioned them. I imagine the demons made enough drivers so that no one would have to wait long before getting picked up."

We plopped through another wall. It was daylight in the new realm, and things seemed more expansive. It seemed as if we were on a quiet country road somewhere, only there was no sky. The outdoors was always an illusion in the demon realms.

"So why are you looking for your grannie?" Dorrie asked.

I tried to judge her expression, but she just focused on the road, seemingly content. "It's a really long story," I answered. "But basically my boyfriend's life depends on me finding her."

Normally someone would focus on the life being in danger part of what I'd said, but apparently not Dorrie. "Oooh, you have a boyfriend?" she asked excitedly. "What's his name? What does he look like?"

I awkwardly answered her questions, and she rewarded me with a brilliant smile as we plopped through another wall.

"I've of course have never had a boyfriend," she explained. "But I find the whole concept of love fascinating. Do you love him? Of course you do," she answered for herself. "If you didn't love him, you wouldn't be trying to save him." A look of stern determination came across her glittering face. "I'm going to help you find your granny," she stated proudly. "And you're going to save your boyfriend. True love is at stake."

We plopped through another wall, a black one this

time. The place we ended up in looked like a scene out of an old Dracula movie. The false sky was a deep indigo, bordered in black and swirling like a storm was brewing. Barren trees reached their feeble limbs up towards that eerie sky like dying animals searching for the touch of the sun. The earth that bordered the road was dark, yet it glistened with moisture that had nothing to do with rain or condensation. The moisture looked thick and slimy, like the remnants of rotting things.

"We're here," Dorrie announced happily.

Of course we were.

Dorrie slowed the cab enough to pull off on the main road onto a bumpy dirt side-road. *Of course.* Of course we had to stop in what looked like the stereotyped version of Transylvania. The demon who had owned the ring could have chosen real estate in the previous sunny realm, but no. Ending up at a creepy old castle would just be the icing on the cake.

The cab bounced violently as Dorrie took the road too quickly. She didn't seem fazed, but I had to hold on to the little strap above the door for dear life as we made our way down the rough road.

Finally we pulled into a driveway and came to a stop. The house in front of us wasn't a castle, but it had the dark, decayed look of a haunted mansion, which was perhaps worse.

"Are you sure this is the right place?" I asked.

Dorrie nodded. "I took this lady home a few thousand years ago. She was wearing that ring, though it was in much better condition at the time."

"A few thousand years!" I exclaimed. "How do you even remember the ring after that long?"

Dorrie rolled her eyes at me. "I was created to navigate and travel through hundreds of realms without a map. My memory is nothing to smirk at bon-bon."

"Sorry," I mumbled as I looked back at the house.

"I'll wait here for you," Dorrie said cheerfully.

"You're not coming?" I asked, knowing the answer but really hoping for the company.

"I'm not supposed to leave the cab," she answered, and for the first time sounded a little sad.

"Who would know?" I asked, now more worried about a creature that could never leave her taxi cab than I was about whatever was in the mansion.

Dorrie seemed to think about it. "I've considered it a few times . . . "

"No time like the present," I said with a wicked grin.

Dorrie leaned forward towards the windshield and observed the mansion. "What if the lady inside tells on me?" she asked, sounding like a little kid.

"What would happen if she did?" I replied.

"They might unmake me," she said sadly. "I've heard of it happening. It's why I've never left the cab before."

I thought about it for a moment. "Maybe you shouldn't . . . "

Dorrie slumped down in her seat dejectedly, but nodded. I felt bad leaving her behind, but I'd probably feel even worse if I got her "unmade". I patted her arm, and had to force myself to not pull my hand away at the sandpaper feel.

Dorrie offered me a small smile. "I'll be waiting right here when you're done."

I exited the cab and strode towards the mansion before I could think better of it. The house was surrounded by a tall, wrought-iron fence that ended at the top with sharp barbs. I took a deep breath and pushed my hands against the partially ajar gate. Dark colored vines had grown over much of the gate, making it difficult to move. I finally ended up just squeezing through the opening that was already there.

The stones that composed the walkway were cracked and edged with the same slimy substance that seemed to cover most of the ground. I did my best to tip-toe across the centers of the stones in order to keep my shoes some-what clean.

The front door looked like it hadn't been opened in ages. What looked like dried slime was caked in the seams and coated the small window in the center of the door. There was no doorbell, so I pounded my fist on the cleanest part of the door a few times. After a few minutes with no answer I knocked a little harder. Still nothing.

I twisted the knob, just to see if the door was locked. It wasn't. I glanced back at the cab and at Dorrie waiting inside. She gestured for me to go ahead, so I turned the knob and the door opened.

"Hello?" I called inside.

No answer.

I pushed the door the rest of the way open, causing dried bits of the slime to flake and fall to the floor. It didn't make much difference. The floor was already caked with the stuff and covered in a layer of dust to boot.

I stepped inside and called out again. Still no answer. I flipped a nearby light switch, but the power was out. I vaguely wondered if demons had to pay electricity bills as I ventured further into the house. I made my way into the expansive kitchen, which was in the same disrepair as what I'd seen of the rest of the house.

The next room was the dining room, which was dominated by a massive, heavy wood table. The table was fully set for guests, but was coated with dust and more crusty slime. Wine glasses that had once been clear crystal were gray with dust.

It took me a moment to realize someone was sitting at the head of the table. She didn't look very old, but had long gray hair and was dressed in black, Victorian style clothing. The thick fabric of her dress was made gray in places by the collecting dust, though there wasn't an ounce of slime on her. She sat slumped in her seat, unmoving.

I could taste my pulse on my tongue as I crept closer to her. Her face was small and delicate, and likely would have been pretty if she didn't look like a corpse.

"Miss?" I questioned, even though I was pretty sure she was dead. I still had to check. If there could be lobster demons, there could be corpse demons.

I leaned on the table to get a little closer to see if she

was breathing. Her hand whipped out and grabbed my wrist, just as her eyes shot open.

She took a deep, rasping breath. "Well," she wheezed. "I've been waiting here all evening." She glared up at me as she chided, "You, my dear are late for dinner."

8
————

"**S**it, sit," she urged. "You must be starving. Of course, if you hadn't of been so late . . . " She rang a tiny bell that had been sitting on the table beside her as if to summon a servant, but no one came.

I cringed as I lowered myself onto one of the dirty chairs. I seriously hoped this woman wasn't my grandmother. If she was, I doubted she'd be of much help to us.

"Oh that dreaded Jessica," my maybe grannie huffed. "That girl is never where she needs to be."

"I've been meaning to ask you about your son," I said conversationally, hoping to get some information out of her as quickly as possible.

She raised her pallid nose up in the air as high as her neck would allow. "You know very well I never had children," she snapped. "That was a very cruel question for you to ask."

"S-sorry," I stammered. "I forgot."

So, she wasn't my grandmother, but she had owned the ring at some point before her. It would have been nice to ask her about it, but if my grandmother had stolen the ring, I might not end up with very much information. It could have been a gift, but this woman didn't seem like the most giving type. I hid my hand under the table so that she wouldn't see the ring just yet.

The woman lowered her nose a bit to look over at me. "I have to say Myrtle, you don't appear much like I remember you."

Crap. "I died my hair," I lied.

The woman tsked. "No, no Myrtle. You don't look at all like you. In fact, you look very much like someone else."

"Someone else?" I questioned nervously.

The woman squinted her eyes at me. "It has just come to me who you look like," she said. "This is a very mean trick to play Myrtle. I demand that you take that face off, or I will have to take it off for you."

I stood and began to back away. The woman stood too, shedding dust like snow onto the floor and table. She took one creaky step towards me, and looked down at my hand.

"You!" she shouted. "You've come back to flaunt that ring in front of me! It was never a fair deal and you know it!"

I backed farther away and prepared to bolt, but suddenly the slime on the floor came to life and enveloped my feet. It slowly made its way up my ankles, and continued creeping. I tried to summon a fireball to throw at the goo, but I was too panicked.

The woman took another step. "I'm going to do something to you, Alexandria, that I should have done years ago," she said slowly.

Alexandria? She had to be talking about my grandmother. She thought I was her. She took another step and raised a hand dripping with slime. I tried to tug my feet free as she took another step and raised the slime covered hand towards my face. Not knowing what else to do, I screamed.

There was a loud crash at the front door that sounded as if it had been blown off of its hinges. Dorrie was suddenly there beside me. She threw out one glittering hand and hit the crazy demon square in the chest. The demon went flying like she'd been hit by a semi, and went right through the far wall of the dining room, leaving a large hole in her wake.

As soon as the woman was out of the room, the slime fell from my feet. Dorrie grabbed my elbow and hurried me through the kitchen and out the front door, which had indeed been blown off of its hinges. We ran down the walkway and back to the cab. As soon as we were inside, Dorrie slammed on the gas and we skidded back down the driveway.

"You left your cab!" I shouted as we pulled onto the main road at top speed.

"I know!" Dorrie shouted back with an exhilarated grin. "I never thought I'd actually do it. It was amazing!"

I couldn't argue that. Dorrie had saved my hide. She turned back to the road and was picking up speed, then suddenly had to slam on the brakes. A slender, tall woman with long blonde hair blocked the way. She stood perfectly at ease as we skidded to a halt just inches in front of her.

The woman tugged her elegant, emerald green trench coat straight and walked calmly to my side of the cab. I slowly opened the door and looked up at her. Green eyes like mine and my dad's looked down at me. Her face was similar to mine, only slightly more angular. She seemed to be a few inches taller than my 5'8" as well. She was my grandmother alright, though she appeared to be in her early thirties.

She smiled. "I could feel that ring from a hundred realms away. Why are you here Alexondra?"

My mouth went dry. "You know who I am?" I squeaked.

"I do," she answered. "Now turn this cab around and go back to where you came from."

With that, she turned and walked away down the road. I jumped out of the cab and followed after the sound of her high heeled boots hitting the asphalt. She somehow stayed ahead of me, even though she was walking and I was running. She was nearing the next realm barrier.

"Wait!" I called out. "I need your help!"

She stopped and looked over her shoulder. The barrier shimmered a dark purple behind her. "What has your father gotten you into?" she asked impatiently.

"It's a long story," I said quickly. "But we need to make a portal. My boyfriend's life depends on it."

Alexandria tsked at me. "Portals are serious business, and whatever happens to your boyfriend, he probably has it coming. Every demon I know has earned their death a thousand times over."

"He's not a demon," I blurted. "Please."

She turned fully around. "Now why would I care about someone who is not a demon?"

"But you just said . . . " I began.

"That all demons deserve their deaths, yes. That does not mean that their lives are not more worthwhile than others," she explained.

I shook my head as my last drop of hope evaporated. She wasn't going to help us. "And to think," I said harshly. "I was actually excited about meeting my grandmother."

She sighed. "As demons, it is in our nature to be self-centered. We are not made to have . . . families." She said the word family like is was distasteful.

"Well I don't care about nature," I said hotly. "I have a family, and Jason is part of it. You may not be willing to help us, but I'll save him anyhow."

I walked back to the cab and got inside. Ignoring my grandmother's tall form staring at us through the windshield, I turned to Dorrie. "Take me home please."

Alexandria walked over and stopped the door of the

cab with her hand before I could shut it. "Give me the ring," she said.

I took it off. "Take it," I said without looking at her. "I'm glad to be rid of it."

She closed her eyes and held the ring in her hand, but her other hand still remained on the door of the cab. After a moment she handed the ring back to me.

"We may not have families," she said without emotion, "but I won't have you tarnishing my good name by fumbling around with lack-luster powers and a broken ring." She snapped her fingers and disappeared in a cloud of smoke.

"What a mean grannie," Dorrie commented once she was gone. She looked at the ring in my palm. "Are you going to put it back on?"

Without a word, I slipped it back on my finger. The ring instantly came to life with flashes of light. The vines on the ring swirled around my finger like tiny serpents. It irritated me that the ring worked now. I just wanted to go back to my body and have this terrible experience over with.

The cab and the earth around it began to shake violently. At first it was just a tremor, then it built into a full blown earthquake.

Dorrie grabbed onto my arm. "What are you doing Xoe!" she shouted.

"Nothing!" I yelled back just as we were both ripped out of the passenger door of the cab and thrown skyward.

Dorrie clung to my arm as the scenery around us

changed with bright swatches of fast moving color. Her rough hands took a good deal of my skin with them as her body was flung away from mine.

I landed on my bed with a bounce, shortly followed by Dorrie who crashed down beside me. "Where am I?" she wailed as she scrambled to right herself.

"Xoe!" Chase said as he rushed into the room. "We were so worried!"

"Was I asleep for long?" I groaned. My head was spinning so violently that I thought I might throw up.

"You disappeared entirely," he said quickly. "You were just gone." He came to sit down beside me just as my dad strode purposefully into the room.

Dorrie clung to my arm once again. "Who are these people?" she whispered nervously. "Where is my cab?"

My dad and Chase both stared at Dorrie as if they had only just noticed her. "You stole a driver?" my dad asked, shocked.

"I didn't mean to," I mumbled. "How is Jason?" I asked before they could lecture me more.

"Xoe," Dorrie whispered, "you have to take me back."

I cringed and looked at her. "I don't even know how we got here in the first place," I said.

"You created a portal," my dad explained. "I don't know how you did it, but it is the only explanation. You did it when you left as well. You were only supposed to go in mind, but your body disappeared."

There was an irritating, throbbing pain between my

eyes. "How is Jason?" I asked again, not liking that they hadn't answered me the first time I'd asked.

"Not good," my father answered simply.

I got to my feet and tried to go for the door. "Don't leave me!" Dorrie exclaimed.

I turned back to her. All I wanted to do was check on Jason, but nothing that was happening was Dorrie's fault. I walked back towards the bed, then grabbed my dad to pull along with me.

"Dorrie, this is my father," I explained calmly. "His name is Alexondre. He's going to stay here with you. We'll figure out how to get you back where you belong as soon as possible."

I didn't see why she was so anxious to go back to a life where she was stuck in a cab all of the time, unless she was just afraid of getting in trouble. I went for the door again, and no one tried to stop me.

I reached the next bedroom to find Jason right where I had left him, but he was not in the same state that I had left him in. He was covered in an electric blanket, yet his skin still felt cold to the touch. Too cold. For the first horrible moment of gripping his hand I thought that he was dead already. I sat in one of two chairs that had been placed beside the bed shakily and looked at his pallid face.

Jason's skin looked a sickly gray, reminding me of the demon who'd tried to kill me with her slime. His eyes shifted slightly behind his closed lids as if he was dreaming. I wondered what type of dreams he might be having, and if his mind knew what state his body was in. I gripped his cold hand a little tighter as tears began to well up in my eyes.

"I can't find it," Jason mumbled, startling me.

His eyes were still shut tight, and I almost thought that I'd only imagined him speaking at all. His eyes shifted once again under his lids.

Jason muttered something that sounded like, "Mother, I can't find the ring."

I stroked my fingers gently across Jason's cheek, willing him to wake up. A gentle knock at the door preceded Allison's entrance. She took the other chair beside me, and put a comforting hand on my shoulder.

"I was going to ask her today," Jason said, more clearly this time.

Allison looked at me in alarm. I looked back at her, not sure what to think. Suddenly Jason's hand flexed in my grip. It flexed again and held on, nearly crushing the bones of my hand. He turned onto his side as he pulled me towards him. He might have been near death, but it seemed he had not lost his vampire-level strength.

"Don't leave me Mary," he said as he clung to my hand. "I'm sorry."

I tried to pull my hand out of his grip. Allison pulled with me, but it was no good. Suddenly he went slack and released me. As I sat back in my chair I realized that at some point I'd started crying again. I wiped at my face as I clutched my bruised hand, but the tears wouldn't stop.

Allison looked startled. "Who's Mary?" she asked breathlessly.

I shook my head. "The poison must be giving him dreams." I turned to fully face Allison, suddenly even more alarmed. "What if it's harming his brain?" I rasped. "What if the damage is unrepairable?"

Allison pulled me into an awkward seated hug. "He's a vampire," she soothed. "He'll heal."

I took a deep, shaky breath. "My dad said that I made a portal. If I can figure out how to do it again, maybe I can make one for Bart. Then he can save Jason."

Allison looked like she wanted to say something, but held back.

"What?" I asked.

Allison shook her head. "It's just . . . how do you know that Bart will actually give you the cure?"

"I won't make the portal until he makes a deal to cure him. Demons don't break deals."

Allison nodded, but still looked unsure. "Once he's free, he just might try and ignore that rule. Especially if you guys are trying to kill him."

"Then I'll make him give me the cure first," I stated as I looked down at Jason.

Allison sighed. "If you say so Xoe. I wish I could be as confident in that fact as you seem to be."

Jason twitched and groaned in his sleep, and I stroked his hair soothingly. I felt an overwhelming surge of adrenaline spurred on by my need to protect him. In that moment I knew with a surety that if I wanted to, I could burn Bart's entire lair down.

Yep. Bart would give me the cure all-right, and then we would kill him. Once Jason was well, I'd make Josie pay for what she'd done . . . that was if I didn't get the opportunity any sooner. In my eyes Josie had earned her death. I was going to save my boyfriend, and then I was going to burn that little witch's world down.

9

Dorrie had recovered slightly since I'd left her. I found her with my dad, helping him mix various liquids into little vials.

"What are you making?" I asked as I walked up behind them.

My dad handed me several vials. "Keep these with you," he said. "We must contain Bart as soon as we release him."

"We have to get the cure for Jason first," I added.

My dad nodded absentmindedly as he handed a mortar and pestle to Dorrie, instructing her to grind the herbs within. "We will do our best to save him," he said, "but our number one priority is containing Bart. We'll need your werewolves to help."

As far as I was concerned, Jason was the number one priority, but there was no point arguing that at the moment. The werewolf part on the other hand . . . "I'm not going to put them in danger," I stated.

"They are in danger regardless," my dad said, still not giving me his full attention.

"Not as much as they would be if I put them around Bart!" I shouted, frustrated that he wasn't fully listening to me.

Dorrie took a few steps back, not wanting to get in the middle of the confrontation. My dad finally faced me. "If Bart defeats us, he will go after them out of spite. This I can guarantee you," he said. "Their chances of survival are far greater if they fight with us."

"Why would he go after them?" I asked, exasperated. "If he kills us, he'll be free to wreak mayhem all across the world."

My dad sighed. "He will see our challenge as a betrayal. He will kill everyone you care about, even if you are already dead. We must face him as a united front, lest we each die one by one."

"You make it sound like we're going to war," I replied.

My dad gripped both of my shoulders. "We may very well be. He managed to recruit Josie, someone Chase trusted. Someone *I* trusted, even if I didn't particularly care for her. I do not know what he promised her, but it's likely he promised the same to others. It may not be just him that we face."

I felt stunned by his words. I hadn't considered that option. "B-but the deal was just for him," I stammered.

My dad let go of my shoulders and turned back to his potions. "Our deal is to give Bart his freedom, but not his safety, so we may still attack him. His only agreement in the deal was to let you go. He is free to try whatever he wishes."

I scoffed. "You demons and your loopholes. Aren't you even going to ask me if I found your mother?" I added.

"She is not with you. That is answer enough," he said. If I didn't know any better. I'd say he almost sounded a bit sad.

I shook my head, though my father couldn't see it. Dorrie had backed even farther into the corner and was watching me nervously like a mouse trapped by two snakes.

"I found her," I replied bluntly. "And she didn't care. She didn't care about Jason, and she sure didn't care about either of us. She fixed the ring and sent me on my merry way."

My dad hunched down as if my words had stung him, and I felt bad for wording things so harshly.

"I thought that perhaps after all of this time . . . " he trailed off. "She fixed the ring you say?"

I held out my hand to him as he turned. He looked down at the ring, but didn't touch it. "Does it feel any different?" he asked.

"Different?" I asked sarcastically. "It was only the catalyst that threw Dorrie and me back into this realm. All I had to do was think of how badly I wanted to be back here and we were suddenly airborne."

My dad looked down at the ring again. "So it's unpredictable . . . yet useful."

I shrugged. "If you say so. How long until we go see Bart?"

I wasn't at all anxious to see the demon, but I was more than a little anxious to get a cure for Jason. It wasn't just to ask him who Mary was, I promise.

"As soon as possible," my dad answered, turning back to his table. "Your vampire doesn't have much time left, and I do not plan on waiting around for another of us to end up in his position. You need to practice and see if you can make a portal to the human world on command. We do not want to get to Bart's lair only to become trapped and at his mercy."

I gawked at him, but he didn't turn around to see. "I don't want to make any more portals than I have to," I said. "I'll just make the one for Bart, and then no more."

He still didn't turn around, but answered. "Just because you have done it twice, doesn't mean that you can do it again. You did not even know what you were doing the first two times. I feel I must repeat that we do not want to end up in Bart's lair without a way to escape."

I knew from previous experience that my dad couldn't just whoosh us out of Bart's lair in a puff of smoke. Bart rarely left his lair for the demon city, and he'd reinforced his surroundings so that others couldn't leave either. It was the whole reason we were in this mess to begin with. My dad had come to my rescue, but once he was there he couldn't get out. Portals were different. They actually tore reality open and let the portal-maker step through.

Before I could argue any further, my dad turned to me. "Take Chase with you. Do not linger in the human world for long. We would not want Bart to discover that you were once again available to him. Just go and come right back."

I glared at him. "I can do it by myself," I argued.

"Just because you can, does not mean you should. Now *go*." He turned back around, effectively dismissing me.

I left the room, slamming the door behind me. I wasn't sure where Chase had gone, so I began wandering the house in search of him. I didn't have to wander far, as he entered the hallway shortly after I did. He stood in front of me with a million emotions running across his face, but he didn't voice any of them.

"Let's go," I said.

He didn't ask where we were going, just followed me into the kitchen. I sat in the middle of the floor and tried to remember how I'd originally made the portal. My heart was pounding with the possibility that I wouldn't be able to do it again, and that I wouldn't be able to save Jason because of it.

I held out a hand to Chase. He took it wordlessly and sat cross-legged next to me. I looked down at our touching knees and intertwined fingers, feeling far too awkward to meet his eyes.

I turned my attention to my other hand, and more

specifically the ring on my finger. I willed it to do something, but it was quiet. I thought back to the flashing lights that it had produced in the cab with Dorrie, and the feeling of being ripped from the car. Still nothing happened.

"Just think of home," Chase instructed.

"Should I click my heels together?" I asked sarcastically.

Chase shrugged. "It couldn't hurt," he suggested.

We both stood. His right hand felt clammy in mine, giving away the fact that he was nervous. I closed my eyes and clicked my heels together while thinking fiercely of home. I imagined myself in my bedroom and could almost feel the worn softness of my comforter.

The room began to shake and I was suddenly overtaken by vertigo. I opened my eyes just as Chase and I were thrown violently into my bedroom. I fell down onto my bed, probably because I'd been thinking of my comforter, but Chase was thrown onto the ground. Before I could say anything, Chase got to his feet and ran into the adjoining bathroom. A moment later I could hear him retching. I only felt a little bit dizzy, but it had apparently affected Chase a great deal more.

He returned to the room a few minutes later, still looking green. "That was nothing like traveling with your dad," he observed.

I got to my feet. "My dad doesn't travel with portals," I replied. I wasn't sure about the mechanics of how my dad traveled, but it definitely wasn't what I had just done.

"We should go back," Chase instructed as he took my hand again.

His hand felt warmer now. I gripped it tightly, worried about accidentally leaving him in my room for Bart to snatch. I closed my eyes and thought about my dad's kitchen, then quickly changed my mind to the bedroom as I remembered our harsh landing. Nothing happened.

I opened my eyes and looked over to Chase. "It's not working."

"We need to get back Xoe, *now*," he answered nervously.

"I know that," I snapped. "But it's not working."

"Don't panic," he instructed. "If we are gone for too long, your father will find us."

Chase telling me not to panic had the opposite effect. Sure my dad would find us, unless Bart found us first. I did *not* want Bart to find us first.

I started to feel faint. "Oh no," I whispered.

Chase grabbed my hands, instantly realizing what was happening. "Fight it Xoe."

"You need to let go of me," I said quickly. "I don't want you to get trapped too! Run!"

Chase pulled me into a tight hug. "I'm not letting you go alone."

I tried to struggle away from him, but then the world shifted. At some point I had closed my eyes, and now I really didn't want to open them. I could still feel Chase with me, holding me tightly against his chest.

"How sweet," a woman's voice commented.

My eyes shot open. I had expected to hear Bartimus, not a woman. From the direction I was facing all I could see were the stone walls of a cave. A familiar smell of damp rock and rotten meat filled my senses. Bartimus' lair was just as I remembered it. I pulled out of Chase's arms in search of who had spoken.

Josie sat at Bart's little tea table as if she hadn't a care in the world. She clutched one tea cup from the set of four delicately in her fingers. Suddenly all I could think about was Jason lying unconscious in bed. Before I knew it I was in front of the table, knocking the antique tea set to the ground as I grabbed for Josie.

I reached for her long, red hair, but came up empty as she dissolved before my eyes only to pop back up a few feet away.

"Ooh," Josie mocked. "She's feisty Chase. I can see why you were always so willing to check on her."

"Stop," Chase demanded, but Josie just rolled her eyes at him. He came to stand beside me.

"You shouldn't have come with me," I whispered.

"Yes," he replied. "I should have."

"Oh such concern," Josie said making an exaggerated sad face. "Don't you even care that your boyfriend is dying, Xoe?"

I flexed my hands, wanting very badly to lash out at her, but I knew she would only evade me again. "You're like one of those annoying little gnats," I said, "that buzz around your head, but you can never quite catch them."

"What did Bartimus offer you?" Chase asked, to

distract Josie from my comment. "You're not trapped down here like he is."

Josie laughed. "When portals start popping up releasing all of the demons, I'd rather be on their side than the humans."

Chase smirked. "You think they'll look out for you because you helped them?" he asked. "I would think you knew better."

"Bart made a *deal* with me," she argued. "I'll be taken care of."

"And what exactly did the deal entail?" he asked smugly.

"He's going to tell the other demons what I've done for them," she said. "If any of them get out of hand, he promised to protect me."

I laughed. "He promised to protect you from other demons, but he didn't promise to not kill you himself."

"T-that's not what he meant," she stammered, finally losing some of her bravado.

I looked over at Chase. "I keep trying to tell everyone that you never make deals with demons."

"You made one!" she snapped. "So don't try and pretend like you're so much smarter than me."

"Yeah, but Bart needs me," I countered. "If he kills me, then I won't be opening any portals. What does he need you for, moral support?"

Josie lifted her nose into the air proudly. "I've already proven myself useful. You would still be at Alexondre's wasting everyone's time if it weren't for me."

I snorted. "You stabbed a vampire. Big whoop. Anyone can hold a knife."

"She has a point," Bart commented as he stepped out of the darkness. His size made Josie look about as big as a teacup poodle, though I thought of her as more of a chihuahua type person. Bart wore a fancy teal colored tuxedo, complete with cummerbund and shiny black shoes. He was all ready for his big day above ground. I was surprised that he could even find a jacket that would fit across his massive shoulders.

"But you promised me," Josie said weakly as she looked up at Bart's imposing form.

Bart edged closer to her. "I know exactly what I promised you, my dear."

"I can still help you," she said just above a whisper.

Bart laughed, and the sound sent chills up my spine. "You are nothing more than a little traitor. You would betray me as well, given the chance. It is in your nature. I would not play the frog to your scorpion."

Bart reached for Josie and Josie didn't even try to fight it. She could have just dissolved again and again, but I knew for a fact that she couldn't get out of his lair without his help, just like my dad couldn't.

"Wait!" Chase shouted as he strode forward.

"Really?" I said under my breath. If it were up to me I would have just let Bart kill her. It would save me the trouble of doing it later.

Bart eyed Chase in amusement. "Correct me if I'm wrong, but I don't think I need you either."

"Well I'm not going to have much luck opening a portal if I'm busy mourning my dead friend," I interrupted with annoyance.

Bart pouted and it looked strange on his large, frightening face. "Well, I'll at least eat the redhead then," he conceded. "I haven't had lunch yet."

Chase looked at me pleadingly.

I let out a loud sigh. "I might be upset about her dying too."

Bart smiled crookedly. "You're lying about that part. You'd be perfectly happy with her dead. I like your style Alexondra. It's a surprise to me that you have any human blood at all."

Josie looked at me like I was a large, angry cat and she was a defenseless little bird. Had she really thought I'd hesitate to kill her? If so, her faith was sorely misplaced. If that made me more of a demon than a human, so be it.

Bart clapped his hands together. "So where is my portal?" he asked. "I've waited more than long enough in this wretched hole."

"We were still preparing," I lied, "but then you went and interrupted us."

Bart giggled. "I know your mind Alexondra. Now make me my portal so I can get on with crushing any who try to stop me."

I had managed to keep our plan of killing him once he got free out of my mind, but him bringing up the idea of someone trying to stop him made me think of it, just for a second. A second was enough.

Bart's smile wilted as he turned his full attention to me. "Be a dear and think that again, would you?"

I laughed weakly. "Just wishful thinking."

Bart offered me a tight-lipped smile that let me know he didn't believe me at all. "We shall see," he replied ominously.

Josie had stepped farther away from Bart and closer to Chase, as if he was the one that had stopped her from being killed. I suppose in a way, he was, and I was fine with him taking credit.

I held out a hand towards Chase and Josie. They started towards me but Bart tsked at us. "No, no," he chided. "No touching the collateral."

"I'm not going to take you through a portal and just leave them here," I scoffed.

"What do you think collateral is? You'll get them back once you deliver," he said reassuringly.

I glared at him, not reassured at all. "You can keep Josie, but I'm not going without Chase. No one can escape your lair without help."

"Xoe!" Chase pleaded, but Bart and I both ignored him for the time being. I'd try and save Josie for his sake, but if it was one or the other, I knew who I was choosing.

"*You* can escape my lair without help," Bart countered. "If you can truly create a portal that is. Once I am safely delivered up above you can come back and get them. Or you can just take the one. It makes no difference to me."

"And you won't interfere?" I asked, needing confirmation.

"My dear," Bart said, oozing charm . . . if giant terrifying demons could be charming. "I will be free for the first time in my centuries long existence. Trust me when I tell you that your little friends will be the last thing on my mind."

I glared at him. "I'll need that in writing," I demanded.

Bart sighed and held up a hand. A moment later a rolled up contract appeared in his meaty palm. "As you wish."

He handed me the contract so I could read it over. When working with demons, one must always read the contract thoroughly. The contract read:

I, Bartimus Vericus Rodmila Delentium, hereby waive all rights to harming those under the protection of one, Alexondra Meyers, on the condition that said party provides a safe portal to the human realm and does not attack me on the other side.

THERE WAS an area on the bottom of the page for both mine and Bart's signatures. Not seeing much of a choice, I held out my hand for the pen Bart was now offering and signed it.

Bart snatched away the contract so he could sign it, then made it disappear in the same way it had originally appeared. He grinned at me proudly. "Now produce my portal," he demanded.

I shook my head. "First the cure for Jason."

"Jason?" he questioned as he twiddled his fingers in excitement.

"My boyfriend . . . the one you *poisoned*," I reminded him.

Bart sighed. "Yes, yes." he snapped his fingers and an old-fashioned black medical bag appeared next to Chase. "After you have delivered you may fetch the cure along with the mongrel demon you seem to care so much about."

Chase didn't look happy about being called a mongrel, but still picked up the bag and gave me a nod. He didn't look happy about the whole situation in general, but unless I was willing to let Bart kill Chase along with Josie, we were out of options.

I looked down at the ring that my grandmother had repaired. The lights in the stone had been dancing like crazy since we'd first entered Bart's magic-filled lair. We were supposed to have a plan of attack before I took Bart anywhere. As it was, my dad wouldn't even know where to wait for us.

Of course, just the fact that he hadn't popped down in an attempt to save us meant he knew what was going on. I'd just have to trust that he'd find us where ever we ended up.

I held out a hand to Bart, definitely not wanting him to touch me, but seeing no other way. He fluttered his meaty palms delicately in the air. "Is the touching necessary?" he asked with distaste.

I rolled my eyes and just continued holding out my

hand to him. Finally he took it, and it was an effort for me to not jerk away. The feel of his skin against mine gave me the chills. I looked down at my ring again, gave a final sarcastic wink to Chase, then thought of the place I'd first almost encountered Bart.

To say the next part was not an easy ride would be a vast understatement. Even though I could in fact cut through Bart's wards with a portal, they weren't going without a fight. We were flung straight up towards the stone of the ceiling, which rather than dissipating as we passed through, melted into a thick, gelatinous consistency.

We wormed our way through in slow motion, for what seemed like hours, but was probably only minutes. Finally we popped out the other side. It seemed like we should have come up from the ground, but instead we fell from the sky into the middle of the woods.

I looked up from where I was lying on the ground in a heap to see the tree that Nick had tied me to right before he planned on slitting my throat. I sat up with a shock when I realized that snow had started to melt through my clothing. After all that had happened, I'd completely forgotten that it was still winter in Shelby. I started to shiver, which was strange since I hadn't really felt the cold since my demon powers had started to grow.

I turned to see Bart lying a few feet away. His large, dark form looked wrong on the fluffy, pristine snow. When he didn't move right away, I thought maybe the fall had killed him and we wouldn't have to worry about doing it ourselves, then he started laughing.

"You brilliant little girl!" he shouted joyfully as he got to his feet and threw handfuls of snow into the air. "I'm free!"

Bart danced around like a puppy playing in the snow for the first time. I almost felt bad that we had to kill him . . . almost.

"Not quite," my dad said as he stepped out from behind a tree and began walking forward, dressed down in a black button up shirt and black slacks. Dorrie was with him, still in her white jumpsuit, but I didn't see any other reinforcements.

Bart sneered at my dad. "You're too late Alexondre. Alexondra has entered into yet another contract with me. You'd think she'd have learned by now that it's not a good idea."

My dad stopped walking and looked at me. "Tell me you didn't," he said tiredly as rubbed at his brow.

"Well," I began, taking a few steps away from Bart, "The contract said that if I made Bart a portal, and didn't attack him myself on the other side, then he wouldn't harm anyone that I would normally protect."

Bart turned his sneer to me. "It didn't specify that only you could not attack-" he began.

"But it also didn't specify that it didn't only mean just me," I interrupted. "Which really leaves things open to interpretation."

Realization played across Bart's face in a montage of

confused, and then angry expressions. If he played by the rules of his own contract, my dad could still attack him, but he couldn't cause harm in return. "That contract was rubbish," he said suddenly. "I don't plan on returning to the underground regardless, so it doesn't matter if I break contracts now."

My dad was beginning to look confident once again. "You know very well that there are others like me with just a trace of human blood. You would be hunted here just as you would down there," he countered.

Bart turned to kick a nearby tree and nearly toppled the thing. He whirled back on my father. "So what? My choice is to die or be hunted? You know which I will choose, Alexondre."

"There is a third choice," my dad stated calmly. "I am willing to offer a new deal."

Bart spat on the ground in irritation. "And what deal would that be?" he growled.

My dad smiled wickedly. "We will take you back underground. Not to your lair of course, but somewhere neutral. All original contracts will be void. You will return to life as you knew it, and so shall we."

I cleared my throat. "Also as part of this contract, we'll be needing back my blood," I added. "All of it."

I looked to my dad for confirmation, and noticed movement behind him. I was about to tell him to look out, but Josie was suddenly there, holding a knife to his throat. Dorrie looked at Josie in horror, as if she couldn't believe that someone had actually attacked us.

"H-how?" I stammered.

Josie laughed and pushed the blade more firmly against my dad's throat. "You tore Bart's wards wide open," she explained. "Once they were gone it was easy for me to escape."

She didn't have to tell me that the blade was poisoned. She wasn't stupid enough to threaten my dad with just a normal blade. "What do you want?" I demanded.

She looked to Bart instead of me when she answered, "I want certain demons to recognize my continued usefulness."

Bart let out a hearty laugh. "Touché little one," he said, then turned to me. "Now Alexondra, if you recall, our contract said nothing about me hurting you, or Josie hurting your father. The only one that cannot do the hurting now ... is you."

10

_____

I glanced at my dad. "Dorrie," he said, voice strained from the knife at his throat. "If you would please assist me, I must help my daughter."

"One little slice will poison you," Josie said harshly with an evil grin on her face.

"Dorrie," my dad said again.

Dorrie looked to me, her sparkly face scrunched in conflict. Bart was matching me step for step as I backed away, obviously enjoying taunting me. I had to turn my attention away from everyone else in order to keep an eye on Bart.

I was absolutely terrified, but I somehow managed to summon a small ball of flame in my palm. It turned the same eerie red as the fire I had summoned in the dream-world. Throwing it at Bart would break the contract, but if my choices were between breaking the contract and dying . . . well my choice wasn't really that difficult. I wasn't even sure if I could hurt a demon with a thrown fireball, but seeing no other choice, I threw the fire.

Bart's eyes widened in surprise right before the fire hit him in the center of his chest and caught onto his clothing. It would have sputtered out quickly, but I focused and was able to will it back to life. Demons could burn after all. Imagine that.

The flame grew quickly and enveloped the majority of Bart's body. He shrieked and fell to the ground in an attempt to put the flames out. The heat caused wet hisses to emit from the snow underneath Bart's thrashing form, yet the fire continued to burn.

I ran away from Bart and back towards where Josie had my dad, summoning another ball of flame as I went.

Josie's eyes darted around in panic before finally settling on my face. "I'll poison him," she threatened. "I took the bag from Chase when I left. There will be no cure for your boyfriend or your father."

"And there will be no cure for *you* after I burn you alive," I replied coldly. "I'd think about your next move very carefully."

Josie suddenly threw the knife and backed away with her hands up. My dad probably would have turned and burned her to death anyway, if it wasn't for the large smoldering presence that I now sensed behind me.

"I don't know whether to kill you now," Bart hissed, "or let you get hunted down for breaking our contract."

I turned slowly, feeling like I was in a horror movie, to look up at Bart. His already charcoal black skin was now raised in welts and blisters. The top half of his fancy suit had been burned away to reveal a monstrous, blistered chest that heaved with a mixture of anger and too much smoke inhalation.

My father and Dorrie came to stand on either side of me. My dad moved his hands in a circular motion and formed a huge ball of flame in his palms. Without warning, he flung it at Bart's face. It hit him square on, but instead of screaming in pain, he disappeared.

I realized the illusion too late as Bart's massive arms wrapped around me from behind. I was encased in the stench of rotten meat and burnt skin as he lifted me off of my feet and walked backwards with me.

"Once you are dead," he rasped in my ear, "there will be no more portals. No one can ever put me back."

He started to squeeze just as my dad and Dorrie started towards us. They were going to be too late, he'd crush me in seconds. My vision was already fading from lack of circulation, so I was pretty sure that my eyes were playing tricks on me as a puff of green smoke appeared right in front of us. The smoke solidified into the figure of a women that seemed to be holding a long object in one hand. The figure leapt, raising the object and slashing it into Bart's neck above me.

His body shuddered as his massive head toppled from his shoulders. Bart's body protected me as the head fell and bounced a few times to finally settle at its owner's feet with a look of shock frozen on its features. I fell out of Bart's arms as his body went limp, then had to rush to the side to not be crushed as his corpse fell forward.

"She's not the only one who can make portals," my grandmother said as she looked down at Bart's body. She was solid now, and looked just as I remembered from our meeting. She held a long, thin sword in her hand and was cleaning it with a green cloth.

"My my grandmother," Dorrie said with a stunned expression on her face. "What strong arms you have."

Alexandria did a double-take at Dorrie, then turned her attention to me. "You stole a driver?" she asked with a glare.

I swayed on my feet and ended up having to crouch on the ground to keep from falling. "It was an accident," I mumbled, feeling sick.

"What's wrong with her Alexondre?" my grandmother snapped.

My dad came to my side and helped me to my feet. "What are you doing here mother?" he asked just as sharply.

Alexandria snorted. "*You* sent the girl to ask for my help," she stated like it was obvious.

My dad held me next to him as he glared at his mother. "And *you* refused."

Alexandria rolled her eyes. "A lady is entitled to changing her mind. Are we done here?"

"Quite," my father answered coldly.

Before I could think to protest, Alexandria snapped her fingers and was gone in a puff of green smoke. I stared at the place where she'd been, feeling like it was all a dream. Then I turned around and looked at Bart's decapitated corpse. Nope, definitely not a dream.

"Not to interrupt," Dorrie chimed in, "but the red-haired girl seems to have disappeared . . . and she witnessed Xoe breaking her contract . . . "

My eyes widened as I turned to look up at my dad. "I'll find her," he stated, but the shakiness in his voice let me know that it really wasn't that simple. "Take Dorrie with you and go find Chase."

"B-but what about Jason's cure?" I stammered.

"Search Bart's lair," he said as he gazed off into the distance. "See what you can find."

He left as quickly as my grandmother had. I turned to look at Dorrie. Her glittery skin and crystalline blue eyes fit in perfectly with our snowy surroundings. It was a shame that she had to go right back to the demon underground, and likely wouldn't have a chance to see the human world again any time soon. I held out a hand to her and she took it gently.

I was worried that I wouldn't be able to get back into Bart's lair, even if I had shattered the wards like Josie claimed. Yet as soon as I closed my eyes and thought of Chase, the cold was whipped away and I landed nearly on top of him.

Dorrie landed on her feet this time. I almost managed it, but Chase had to catch me as I teetered on my feet for a moment, then stumbled forward.

Chase's face betrayed the million questions he held

inside, but there would just have to be time for that later. "Where's the bag?" I asked quickly. "Josie said she took it."

Chase's gaze shifted to the ground beside his feet, and relief flooded me as I saw the bag. "She tried to grab it," he explained, "but I was prepared. Trusting her didn't work out well for me the last time."

"Sorry," I mumbled, finally feeling a little guilty about blaming him for Josie's actions.

"Xoe-" he began.

"There's no time," I cut him off. "Let's see how this portal thing works with three people."

Chase picked up the medical bag as I grabbed onto his free hand and offered my other hand to Dorrie. She took it, and I closed my eyes once again, thinking of my dad's home.

We ended up in my dad's kitchen, and I immediately took the medical bag from Chase and ran to Jason's room. He was right where I left him.

I opened the bag to find a single syringe inside, filled with a dark red liquid. I handled it gingerly as I held it up to the light, then looked at Jason. I wasn't sure if I should just inject him in the side of his arm, or if it needed to be intravenous. My eyes widened as another thought came to me. What if it was similar to an adrenaline shot and needed to go into his heart? I started feeling dizzy at the thought.

Finally I decided that getting the cure in his bloodstream would be the best bet. I walked to the bed and sat down next to Jason, who was in a deep sleep that seemed eerily close to death. My heart raced as I searched for a vein in his inner arm. I had to hold my breath while I slid the needle home, and still my hands shook slightly. I emptied the dark fluid into his vein, then pulled the syringe out. I watched as a tiny bubble of liquid followed the needle out of his arm, then turned to look at his face. Nothing happened.

I don't know why I expected an instant cure in the first place, but it would have been nice if there was some small change to tell me that the antidote had worked. Instead, Jason remained completely still. His skin was icy and there were dark purple bruises under his closed eyes.

I started to cry just as Allison walked into the room, holding a fabric-covered hot water bottle in her hand. "Xoe!" she exclaimed. Her surprised expression quickly shifted to anger. "How could you just go off like that?" she chided. "I was stuck down here with your mom while she had hysterics."

I turned my attention back to Jason. "Where is my mom now?" I asked distantly as I placed my hand against Jason's neck. Did his skin feel even colder?

"She's back in Shelby," she explained. "Your dad came back here first and tried to run right off again, but your mom made him take her home."

I finally turned back to face her. "S-she left?" I squeaked.

Allison's expression softened. "This has all been really hard on her-" she began.

"She could have at least waited to see for herself that I was okay," I mumbled.

Allison walked closer, but then gave me a wide berth as she went to lay the hot water bottle against Jason's neck. I turned a hurt expression towards her.

"Sorry," she said dejectedly as she sat down beside me with a huff, "but you *do* tend to get randomly angry a lot lately, and I can't heal as well as everyone else."

I nodded, but didn't reply. I couldn't really blame her for being cautious.

"So you got the antidote?" Allison asked. "Did you already give it to him?"

I nodded numbly, and slumped against Allison as she put an arm out to comfort me. "He doesn't look any better," she commented honestly, "but maybe it just takes time."

I nodded again, utterly exhausted and unable to think of anything to say, and we sat like that for a very long while.

11

Eventually Chase came into the room to join us. He took one look at Jason, then sat wordlessly on the floor to wait. My dad still hadn't returned from hunting down Josie, which was probably a very bad sign.

I'd broken a contract with another demon. It was a grave offense. I tried to be frightened by the possibility of being tortured to death by demons, but all of the fear I had was focused on the possibility of Jason dying. Once he was awake, then I could worry about demons. For the time being, I was just worried about his icy-cold stillness.

At one point Dorrie had come in with a plate of food, but I refused to eat. Even just thinking about food made me queasy. I could somehow sense it when night mercifully fell. I curled up next to Jason's cold form and slipped into the deepest sleep of my life. If I dreamed, I didn't remember them, and it was probably a good thing.

I woke to someone gently stroking my hair. At first I thought that my mom had come back, because that was how she often woke me when I was younger. I opened my eyes to find Jason looking down at me with a soft smile. My mom would have been nice, but at that moment Jason was so much better. He still looked like death, but his eyes were open, and that was good enough for me.

"Good morning," he said softly as he continued to look down at me.

I shot up in bed, feeling so many emotions that I didn't know which one to feel first. "It worked!" I exclaimed. "How do you feel?"

Jason cringed. "I have not felt this bad since I had the flu when I was human."

"Well at least you're alive," I said with a smile.

"If you say so," he said jokingly. "Would you mind telling me what happened?"

It was my turn to cringe. He'd missed a lot. I started by telling him he'd been poisoned, then I explained the events following said poisoning. He was not happy when I got to the part about Josie disappearing with knowledge that could very well condemn me to death.

His eyes widened in panic as I explained to him that our only chance was if my father could find Josie before she ratted me out. "We have to hide," he blurted out. "Your father said-"

I dropped my head back down to my pillow with a sigh. "Josie is the *only* witness," I explained. "At least the only witness that would turn me in, and my dad is looking for her. It'll be fine."

"But what if he cannot find her?" he said, still obviously panicked. "We need to be prepared. We shouldn't just wait down here for the other demons to find out."

"Hey Jason," I interrupted, not wanting to talk about my impending doom any longer. "Who's Mary?"

"M-mary?" he stammered. "What do you mean?"

I turned my head away, suddenly embarrassed that I'd even felt the need to ask. Jason leaned over me and stroked my hair back from my face, waiting for me to speak.

"You talked about her when you were unconscious," I mumbled, still not looking at him. "You said that you were going to marry her."

Jason's hand paused against the side of my face, and then he slowly took it away. "I was," he admitted, "but it was a very long time ago. Does that upset you?"

I shrugged my shoulders against the bunched up comforter. "No. Yes . . . I guess I was just shocked that you never told me."

"It was a very long time ago," he explained. "A very, *very* long time ago. I didn't think it was relevant."

I finally turned to face him. "Did you ever find the ring to ask her?"

Jason nodded. "I found it. I was going to see her that evening, but Maggie found me first."

My stomach did a little nervous flip. Maggie was the vampire who'd turned Jason. I'd been slightly instrumental in her death, though she'd been trying to kill me so I didn't really feel bad about it.

"Maggie took me and turned me," he explained. "She kept me with her for several days. She convinced me that I could no longer have my human life, I told her that I at least needed to see Mary to say goodbye. It wasn't fair to simply disappear. Maggie agreed. At the time I thought she was being kind, but eventually I realized that she knew exactly what would happen. She did not send me to Mary out of kindness. She sent me out of cruelty."

When he didn't speak, I nuzzled closer to him. "You hurt her," I said softly.

"I killed her," he corrected. "I went back to Maggie with Mary's blood on my mouth and left my home behind."

"What about your mother?" I asked, remembering him speaking to her as he frantically searched for Mary's ring.

He pulled me into the circle of his arms. "I couldn't risk seeing her," he explained. "I did go back many years later, after I had left Maggie and learned to control myself, but my mother had died. I never went back again."

"I'm sorry," I whispered, not sure of what else to say.

Jason nodded. "It is the past, and you are my present and future. I am much more worried at the moment about demons taking you away and torturing you to death."

There was a knock on the door, but before I could get

up to answer it, Allison let herself in. She looked flushed, and her normally perfect honey blonde hair was a flyaway mess. She was in jeans and a plain white tee-shirt, which was extremely under-dressed for Allison.

"I tried to stop him," she blurted out quickly.

I straightened up in bed. "What now?" I said tiredly.

"Chase thought your dad should have been back by now," she explained as she stepped closer. "It's good to see you awake Jason," she added, as if she had only just noticed that he was no longer comatose.

Jason nodded and Allison continued, "Chase thought something might have happened, so he went looking for Josie."

I slumped back down in bed, feeling tired and about eighty years old. "Did he say where he was going to look?" I asked as I numbly stared at the far wall.

"Let your father and Chase handle it," Jason interrupted, knowing where my mind was going. "It's not your job to take care of everyone."

I snorted. "Could have fooled me."

"He didn't say where he was going," Allison added, "and I agree with Jason."

"Well Josie already almost killed Jason," I countered. "I can't just sit back with the possibility that she might hurt my dad or Chase."

"Your dad can take care of himself," Jason said sternly, "and he got you into this whole mess to begin with. Let him sort it out."

I struggled up out of bed, feeling frustrated that

no one was supporting me. If the situation was reversed, my dad and Chase would be out looking for me, no matter whose fault the situation was. Heck, they were both out there looking for Josie because of me. Really, I should have been the one finding her.

"Xoe please," Jason pleaded. "I'm not even sure if I'm able to stand right now. I can't protect you."

That stopped me, not because I needed Jason to protect me, but if I left I wouldn't be able to protect him. "Gather your things," I said turning to Allison.

"W-what?" she stammered.

"Just do it," I ordered.

Allison left the room without another word. Jason watched me thoughtfully, wondering what I was up to. Knowing he would argue with me if I explained, I chose to pace the room in silence until Allison returned.

She had to turn sideways and shuffle through the doorway in order to fit her large suitcases through all at once. Once inside, she dropped her baggage onto the carpet with a huff.

"Over next to Jason," I ordered.

She obeyed, though her exaggerated noises of effort let me know that she wasn't happy about being bossed around. I went to stand in between Allison and Jason. I lifted Jason's hand off of the bed and entwined my fingers with his, then held out my free hand to Allison.

She glared at my outstretched palm. "I can't hold both suitcases in one hand," she stated grumpily.

"Well then we'll just have to come back for one later," I sighed. "Pick the more important one."

Allison gave me a *yeah right* look.

"Allison," I began harshly.

"Fine!" she interrupted and grabbed the larger of the two suitcases.

I grabbed her free hand and thought of home, but instead of the upward motion of my previous portals, the room began to shake violently.

"Is this supposed to happen!" Allison shouted over the rumbling of the house.

"Just don't let go of my hand!" I shouted in reply as I tried my hardest to keep my thoughts on home.

Suddenly we were ripped violently towards the ceiling, and it was all I could do to hold onto Allison and Jason's hands. We ended up sprawled in the snow. I sat up and was flooded with relief as I saw my house. For a moment I thought maybe I had put us in the middle of the woods, but I'd only actually missed my destination by a little bit. The earthquake still had me worried though. My portals seemed to be getting worse rather than better.

There was a groan to my left and I turned just in time to see Allison vomit on the fresh snow. She spat onto the ground and turned her face towards me. "I hate you," she groaned.

"I know," I said as I got to my feet. I had to help Jason stand, and with his full weight on me I almost fell back down. The lack of food in my system was beginning to make me dizzy.

Allison slowly got to her feet and went to Jason's other side. With her help we were able to drag him into my house. My stomach was full of butterflies at the thought of seeing my mom, but she wasn't there. We sat Jason down onto the couch, then I picked up the phone to call Lucy.

"Would you care to tell me what you're planning?" Allison said as she came to stand in front of me with her hands on her hips.

I shook my head and mumbled, "No."

Just as Allison was about to say more, Lucy answered. I quickly explained everything that had happened, then without waiting for Lucy's reaction said, "I need you and Max to come here and look after Jason and Allison."

"Xoe!" Allison argued as she realized I was still planning on going after Josie. Jason was silent. He probably had known all along.

I hung up the phone. "You guys shouldn't stay here," I said, ignoring Allison's frantic expression. "We don't need to make it any easier for . . . anyone to find you."

Really, I didn't know if Jason and Allison were in any danger. Josie might try to hurt them, but it wouldn't make any sense for her to do so. She already had all of the leverage to hurt me that she'd ever need. I was more worried about her telling the other demons what happened, and them sending half-demons to look for me.

It would have been nice to know where my mom was so I could tell her to leave as well, but it didn't seem as if she'd spent much time in the house. I rushed through the kitchen for any sign that someone had eaten there. The remaining coffee in the coffee pot was dry and sticky, and the trash under the sink seriously reeked.

There were a few dirty dishes, but the dried, crusty food on them told me that they were from before we had left. Allison followed me as I went up the stairs and into my mom's room. The bed wasn't made, but that wasn't anything new. Other than that, I couldn't find anything to tell me whether or not she'd been there.

I turned around abruptly to face Allison. "My dad brought her back here, right?"

"Y-yeah," she stammered. "I saw her before they left."

I gestured behind me to the empty bedroom. "So where is she?" I asked breathlessly as I began to panic.

"I'm sure she just went out," she said softly.

I stretched my neck from side to side to relieve some tension as I competed with the overwhelming need to act. "When Lucy and Max get here, you have them take you somewhere else. Abel and his recruits are still in town. If Lucy protects you and Jason, the others will be obligated to protect her."

"Xoe," Allison said softly. "You just need to stay with us."

I shook my head back and forth and little too quickly. "I can't just sit here. I don't know where my mom, dad, or Chase are. I have to *do* something."

I pushed past her and went back downstairs to find Jason using the couch as a support to keep himself standing. "Sit back down," I ordered.

"You're not going without me," he replied through gritted teeth.

I walked over to him and guided him back down to the couch. "I did *not* go to all of the effort of saving you just to have you overexert yourself and ruin it all," I chided.

Jason pulled me down onto the couch with him and forced me to meet his eyes. "Please don't go," he begged. "I cannot deal with you putting yourself in constant danger like this."

"It's not like I chose to live this way-" I began.

"It is a choice though," he replied. "You didn't have to get involved with the werewolves, and that led to everything else. You need to stop trying to save everyone."

I pulled away from him so that I could turn my gaze down to my lap. "It's just how I am," I mumbled, but the response sounded weak even to me.

Jason sighed and leaned back fully onto the couch. "Sometimes we have to change in order to survive," he said softly. "I am not the person I used to be."

I looked at him as a lump of anxiety began to build in my throat. "You would change who I am?" I asked, truly shocked.

"Sometimes Xoe," he said dejectedly. "I think I would."

"You would seriously have me stay here and not help my dad and Chase?" I pressed, not wanting to believe what I was hearing.

"Don't you see that they're trying to protect *you*?" he blurted out in frustration. "Why can't you let them?"

"They could *die*," I said harshly. "And then I would have to live with the fact that I did nothing to help them."

"And if I let you go now," Jason countered, "and something happened to you, I'd have to live with that fact as well."

"There is no *letting* me go," I snapped. "Whether I go or stay is my choice. This is my *dad* we're talking about here. It's family. Heck, for all I know, Josie could have taken my mom as bait for whatever scheme her twisted mind has come up with now."

"And Chase?" Jason prompted. "What about him?"

I took a deep breath and let it out. "He's risking his life for me. You can't ask me not to do the same for him."

"Well I am asking you," Jason replied simply.

I felt like I was going to cry, but I forced myself to hold back. "And I'm saying no," I answered quietly.

It would have been nice to just say okay, and stay nice and safe with Jason, but I couldn't. I just couldn't. It wasn't right to let others risk their lives because of me. All of my dad's problems were because of me, yet he continued to look out for me. Chase could have left all of the danger behind at any point, but he had stayed. It wasn't right to let them shoulder all of the risk.

I stood to leave, feeling terrified and offended all at the same time. Terrified at the prospect of Jason getting fed up with me and leaving, and offended that he really thought I could abandon the people taking care of me.

I fought back the tears that tried to well up in my eyes, and it was one of the most difficult battles I had faced. Just because I knew that I was making the right choice, didn't make it any easier. The expression on Jason's face as my decision sank in made things harder still.

Yet, no matter what Jason wanted, I couldn't just leave the people trying to protect me on their own. It wasn't fair, and they wouldn't leave me if the situation was reversed. Apparently that made me hard to love. So be it. I had plenty of other good qualities.

12

Lucy and Max had shown up with a few other wolves in human clothing, but unfortunately there was no time for a big reunion. The wolves that I didn't know demanded that I tell them everything that was going on so that they could report to Abel. I ignored them until they demanded that I go with them. I told them to make me, and they backed down.

Jason grabbed my wrist as I helped him into the large SUV the wolves had driven. "Please Xoe," he said one last time, "just come with us."

I shook my head. "You know I can't."

He shook his head in return and sat back against his seat. Apparently I wasn't getting a goodbye kiss.

I backed away so he could close the car door, then watched forlornly as the SUV drove away. I started to shiver, which was a strange phenomenon for me, given that I hadn't really felt the cold in months. Yet I felt it right in that moment, as if it would freeze my very bones until they cracked. I shook away the imagery and went back inside my empty house.

Lucy was going to try and scent out my mom, so I either needed to go after my dad or Chase. Chase couldn't travel like my dad and I could, so he would probably be the easiest to find. In fact, he was likely still in the demon city, looking for signs of Josie.

I closed my eyes and thought of my dad's house. My living room began to shake and I almost lost my concentration, then I had a moment of being airborne before everything went black. The next thing I knew, I was opening my eyes and there was a terrible pain in my side.

I slowly sat up as I gripped at the pain. My hand came away with blood. Shocked, I observed my surroundings. The room I was in looked sort of like my dad's kitchen, but everything was destroyed. The stools were little more than broken shards, and many of the tiles were jutting upward like something large had pushed its way through them. One of the tiles was what had stabbed my side. I held my hand against the wound as I got to my feet. Everything was still and silent, except I could hear a distant sound like someone crying.

I stumbled across the broken floor and into the hallway. The light fixture had been ripped partially out of the wall and was flickering on and off ominously. Blood was beginning to seep through my fingers to drip onto the mostly shredded carpet, leaving a morbid trail behind me.

The crying sound got louder as I neared the bedroom where Jason, Allison, and I had departed from. The room was dark, but I could make out a glittering white form huddled in the corner.

"Dorrie!" I exclaimed as I realized what I was seeing.

Dorrie lifted her head out of her hands. "Xoe?" she questioned, sounding like she didn't quite believe it was me. "W-when you left I thought-"

"I'm sorry," I interrupted. I was glad that it was dark enough that she probably couldn't see me blushing from embarrassment. "There was just so much going on that I forgot-"

"Well you remembered now," she said with a soft smile. "Thanks for coming back for me pork chop."

I didn't have the heart to tell her that she wasn't the reason I'd come back. Instead I asked, "What on earth happened here? It looks like a tornado passed through."

Dorrie rose shakily to her feet. "I think it happened when you left," she explained. "I was just coming to find you, and the whole house started shaking. I opened the door just in time to see you disappear."

"I'm sorry Dorrie-"

"You're bleeding!" she interrupted as she darted towards me.

"Dorrie," I said, cringing as she ripped my hand away from the wound to take a look at it. "Did you say all of this happened because of us leaving?"

She nodded somberly. "I think something is going wrong with your portals pot pie."

I cringed, and not from the pain this time. The earth had shook when I left my mom's house too. I had a sickening feeling that destroying my mom's entire house like I'd apparently done to my dad's would *not* help things with our relationship.

"Dorrie," I began again, pulling my wounded side away from her, "I need to find Chase."

"Your granny was here," she said, too sidetracked by pushing a stray tee shirt against my wound to listen to me. "She felt your portal and came to see what went wrong."

"And she just left you here?" I asked, exasperated.

Dorrie shrugged. "No offense, but your granny isn't very nice. She went off in a huff when I told her I didn't know where you'd gone."

"Of course," I grumbled as Dorrie finished tying a second, torn-up tee shirt around my waist.

Dorrie straightened back up and looked down at her handy work. "You sure are a gangly little thing," she commented.

"Gee thanks," I replied sarcastically.

"Sure," she said, not catching my sarcasm. "So you need to find Chase? He's the cute tall one right?"

"Sure," I replied, mimicking her tone. "He left before us, but he can't create portals or travel like my dad does, so I think he's still down here somewhere."

Dorrie suddenly looked worried. "I can't go out there with you poppy seed," she said sadly. "I'll be caught and unmade."

I bit my lip, feeling guiltier than ever. "I have to find

Chase," I explained, "but I promise I'll come back here for you and put things right. Don't be scared."

Dorrie nodded, though her glittery eyes shone with unshed tears. "Please hurry," she said softly.

I turned to leave, but she pulled me into a fierce hug before I could take two steps. I gasped in pain as the movement strained at the wound in my side. Dorrie instantly released me with an apologetic cringe. I forced a smile, though the entire left side of my body was on fire, and turned to go once again.

"Be safe!" Dorrie called down the hallway as I reached the kitchen.

I went through the kitchen and stopped in the entry room to paw through the coat closet. The entry room was surprisingly intact, as if the destruction of my portal could only reach so far. Finally I found a dark blue zip-up hoodie that I highly doubted belonged to my father.

Judging by the way it fit me as I pulled it over my arms, it belonged to Chase. Whatever. It would cover my wound, and maybe it would bring me luck in finding him. I pulled the zipper most of the way up my chest and tugged the hoodie forward to cover my hair and shadow my face.

I took a deep breath and went outside, expecting for some reason to be instantly accosted, but I was greeted with an empty street. I set off at a fast pace, ignoring the pain in my side and the protests from my empty stomach. Walking was a difficult task, as I felt incredibly weak, and

I could also feel the blood beginning to seep through Dorrie's makeshift bandages.

Once I reached the more populated area of the city, I began asking some of the younger-looking demons if they knew Chase or had seen him. Most of them just gave me strange looks and walked away, and one completely normal looking boy hissed at me as he whipped his forked tongue out towards my face.

Feeling defeated, I went and sat on the front steps of the large, golden library. My dad had a way of finding me no matter where I was, but unfortunately the ability didn't seem to be hereditary.

Someone came and sat down beside me, and I was shocked when I turned to see Josie's smiling face. She grabbed my wrist and pulled me up to my feet. I struggled, but she pulled me close to her like we were the best of friends, and I was too weak from blood loss to fight her.

"There's no need to cause a scene," she said pleasantly. She dragged me forward, then down a nearby deserted alleyway.

I looked back over my shoulder as the busy street disappeared from view, then turned around as we turned a corner that put us behind the library. I didn't like being alone with Josie in my weakened state. Well, I didn't like being alone with her regardless, but being helpless made things that much worse.

"What do you want?" I snapped as I tried to hide the fact that I was about to fall over.

"I want what any self-respecting demon wants," she replied. "Power."

"Let me rephrase that," I said, letting my annoyance show clearly in my tone. "What do you want from *me*?"

"Well, my first plan died with Bart," she said as she causally looked around us for any passersby. "So I've devised a new one. You're going to make portals for the more powerful demons, and I'm going to reap all of the benefits."

I snorted. "I don't think so."

Josie's smile disappeared from her face. "You don't seem to know how this blackmail thing works. Also, are you aware that you're bleeding?"

I followed her gaze down to the small trickle of blood that was forming on the side of my jeans. Ignoring the blood, I turned my gaze back to Josie. "Where are Chase and my father?" I demanded.

"I don't know where Chase is," she answered, "but your dad is trying to wait me out at the courthouse. He thinks I plan on reporting you for breaking your contract, but what would I gain from that?"

I let out a breath of relief that made my side ache. "And what's to stop me from just killing you to shut you up?" I pressed.

"My brother knows what you did. If I go missing, he'll go right to the court. I know you're new around here, so you should know that the court has ways of making you tell the truth. If they question you, you're cooked."

I was beginning to feel dizzy with blood loss. "And

what if I just kill your brother?" I asked, trying to keep the pain out of my voice.

"I don't think that will be necessary," someone said from behind us.

Josie and I both turned to see Verril leaning against the wall of the library and looking quite smug.

"You idiot!" Josie chided, "You're supposed to be a thousand miles away from here right now."

"And you're supposed to be my sister," he countered hotly.

"What is that supposed to mean?" Josie snapped as she stood to face him.

"It means, dear sister," Verril replied, pausing between words for dramatic emphasis, "that I'm about to pay you back for leaving me to deal with the consequences of your schemes, yet again."

"They wouldn't have hurt you," Josie said, rolling her eyes.

I raised my hand weakly. "I would have."

"I can't blame you," Verril said pleasantly as he finally turned to acknowledge me. "And I'm here to tell you that you don't have to worry about me turning you in. My sister is going to get me killed one of these days. I'll be much better off if she just gets killed instead."

"Verril!" Josie gasped.

Josie looked at her brother in horror. When he didn't assuage her fears, her expression turned to anger. "Well I suppose I'll just have to go straight to the courts after all," she snapped. "We'll let your father try and stop me," she added, turning towards me, "and he'll go down with you."

She started to dissipate, but Verril darted forward and grabbed her wrist. Instantly she became solid again. Josie looked at her brother with tears in her eyes. "She'll kill me," she whispered up at him.

"No she won't," another voice said as a figure stepped around the corner.

The figure's face was hidden underneath the hood of his black sweatshirt as he approached Verril and Josie. Josie looked up at the face underneath the hood and smiled. "I knew you wouldn't let anything happen to me," she said.

I started backing away from the scene, not liking the odds of Verril and I standing against Josie and the newcomer. I froze in my tracks though as the figure stabbed a knife into Josie's stomach and up underneath her ribs. Josie let out a harsh grunt of surprise.

I finally recognized Chase's voice as he said, "I didn't mean that I was going to save you from her. I just meant that I was going to kill you first."

Josie stared up at Chase as her body slumped forward. Chase pulled the knife away, and Verril caught his sister's body as she fell. The two men stared at each other for a moment, then Verril nodded and lifted his sister's body into his arms. He turned and nodded towards me as well, then backed away farther into the network of alleyways.

Chase rushed to my side and caught me just as I was

about to fall to my knees. "You're injured," he observed worriedly.

"And you're holding a knife covered in the blood of the woman you just murdered," I commented back as the sides of my vision began to go gray.

Chase dropped the knife to the ground like he'd just realized he was holding a venomous snake. We both stared at the bloody knife on the ground, then I summoned a weak fireball into my palm. I almost missed as I threw it at the knife, melting it into an indistinguishable puddle.

"Are you upset that I killed her?" he asked, incorrectly reading my expression.

"I'm more worried about how it might affect you," I admitted as I let most of my weight fall against him.

"It had to be done," he said sadly. "We could have all died and she wouldn't have batted an eye. She was evil. Even her brother agreed."

"Why the change of heart?" I pressed. "In Bart's lair you seemed pretty bent on saving her."

Chase shook his head. "That was before she had the power to turn you into the courts. They can never find out about what happened."

I didn't know what to say to that, so instead I asked, "So you worked with Verril to find Josie?"

Chase nodded as we began to hobble forward. "He came to me as soon as she told him her plan. This wasn't the first time she'd betrayed him to better her own standing."

We walked in silence for a while. Well, Chase walked and basically dragged me along. "You cared about her once," I commented. I wasn't sure why I said it. Probably the blood loss.

"Well I care about you more," he said quietly.

I pulled him to a stop, and he turned a concerned gaze to me. "What's wrong?" he asked. "Are you going to pass out?"

I put my hands on either side of his face and did something that I would never admit to thinking about on several occasions. I pulled his face down and kissed him. At first he was surprised, then kissed me back. I felt my last bit of strength leave me as I pulled away.

He looked down at me, completely shocked. "I'm going to assume that was the blood loss," he said, though he smiled while he said it.

"Yes," I mumbled. "Blood loss," and then I fainted.

13

Chase got me home and left me with Dorrie while he went and found my dad at the courts. I woke up in the middle of my dad stitching up my side, and called him around ten different bad names before passing back out again.

The next time I woke up, I was in the bedroom that I had stayed in when we first arrived at my dad's house. Most of the debris had been cleaned up, though the walls and floors were still thoroughly damaged.

I was surprised to see Allison sitting on the foot of my bed. She turned to look at me as I sat up.

"What are you doing here?" I croaked, then had to swallow a few times to get the sandpaper feeling out of my throat.

"It's nice to see you too, Xoe," she said softly in reply.

"What's wrong?" I asked, worried by her tone.

"Your dad thought it would be best if I told you-" she began.

"Told me what?" I interrupted as I gathered my legs to my chest. We'd gotten rid of Bart and Josie. Everyone was supposed to be safe.

"Your mom wants you to live with your dad for a while," she said with an apologetic look. "She thinks maybe with all of the recent danger, he can take care of you better than she can."

"She doesn't want to see me?" I asked as tears welled up in my eyes.

"Of course she wants to see you," she said, though she didn't sound very convincing.

"Where's Jason?" I asked morosely, not wanting to think about the situation with my mother right at that moment.

"He's in Shelby, just to make sure that the danger has passed. Able went back to Utah," she explained.

I was glad that he was looking after things, though I couldn't help but feel like maybe he didn't want to see me either. It seemed I was losing popularity points by the second.

"I kissed Chase," I said suddenly, needing to admit it to someone. "But it was after a great deal of blood loss."

Rather than commenting, Allison scooted up on the bed to snuggle her shoulder against mine companionably.

"Are you hungry?" she asked after we had sat in silence for a while.

"Starved," I replied with what could almost be considered a smile.

Allison scooted down the bed and slid off to stand. "I won't tell anyone about Chase," she said, "but you should probably make up your mind at some point. It's getting a bit ridiculous."

"I know," I mumbled miserably as I looked down at my lap.

Allison nodded, as if my answer satisfied her. She turned to leave the room, but paused in the doorway and looked back at me with a wicked smile. "So how was it?" she asked.

I sighed. "It was fantastic," I answered sadly.

Allison nodded, and turned to leave again, though I'm pretty sure I heard her say, "Thought so," as she left.

Allison returned a short time later. We spent the rest of the evening eating demon-made pizza and watching bad movies on the new laptop my dad had come home with to replace the one that was destroyed along with the rest of his things.

My dad wasn't happy about his house, but was blaming himself more than he was blaming me. Although, the person that he blamed the most was his mother, for reasons unbeknownst to me. For the time being, I was just going to let my father deal with Alexandria. I had enough going on already.

I knew I still needed to deal with my malfunctioning portals, my probably totally freaked out mother, Jason, my werewolf pack, and a myriad of other things . . . but I'd deal with them all tomorrow . . . or maybe the day after that. If anyone asked, Allison would just have to tell them I was on vacation.

ABOUT THE AUTHOR

For more information, please visit www.saracroethle.com!

SNEEK PEEK AT BOOK FIVE!

"So how does it feel to be a high school drop-out?" Chase asked as we both stared at the ceiling.

I squinted at the white plaster, then arched my back slightly, trying to find a more comfortable position on the carpet. "I just keep hearing every teacher and adult I've ever known telling me that high school drop-outs are destined to become life-long failures."

Chase turned his head and laid his cheek against the carpet so he could look at me. "You're going to get your GED. That's all I have."

I snorted as I let my head drop over to face him. "You're twenty-two and you don't even have a job."

Chase glared. "I work for your father. That's a job."

I laughed and turned my attention back up to the ceiling. "All you have to do is hang out with me. That is *not* a job."

"That's debatable," Chase replied. "Since we met I've

been bitten by a vampire, held hostage in the lair of a psychotic, cannibalistic demon, and I killed my ex-girlfriend. Xoe, you are a lot of work."

I sighed. "At least I'm charming enough to make up for it all."

Chase laughed. "Also debatable."

My dad appeared in the doorway of Chase's room, causing us both to lift our heads from the carpet to look at him.

He looked down at me with green eyes the exact color of my own, and crossed his arms, wrinkling the corners of his pricey dress-shirt in his best responsible parent impression. "You should be studying, Xoe. You're going to take that test whether you like it or not."

I let my head fall back to the carpet with a soft thud. "I suffered through two and a half years of high school, only to come away with nothing. Let me mourn in peace."

"It was *your* choice to drop out," my dad replied, his words heavy with disapproval.

"I live in the demon underground, my mother barely speaks to me and doesn't want me in her house, my boyfriend has disappeared, and . . . I just can't go back there," I finished.

"You've still heard nothing from him then?" my dad asked, replacing his disapproval with sympathy.

My arms scratched across the carpet as I shrugged my shoulders on the ground. "Not since I forced him into a vehicle full of werewolves so he wouldn't get himself killed."

Chase moved his elbow across the ground to nudge my arm. "Jason loves you," he comforted, though there was a hitch in his voice as he said it. "He'll come back."

I closed my eyes and tried to turn off the strange feelings pulsing through my mind. I'd never been an anxious person, but in the past few months, I'd learned what true anxiety felt like. I took a deep breath and tried to think of a reply for Chase. Normally I'd be having such a conversation with Lucy and Allison, but with them busy with school and normal life, Chase and my dad had to be my stand-in girlfriends. They tried, but couldn't quite fit the bill.

I pictured Allison in my head. Given the chance, she would tell me to stop whining, and Lucy would be hard at work figuring out a solution to my problems. If the boys had taken some lessons from the girls, I probably wouldn't still be moping about on a bedroom floor of questionable cleanliness.

"You both need to get up and get out of this house," my dad announced.

With an exaggerated sigh, Chase stood, towering over my prostrate form at 6'1". He offered me a hand up, which I took grudgingly. We then stood looking at my dad, waiting for an explanation.

My dad rolled his eyes. "*Go*. I will not harbor slugs in my house."

"Gee dad, love you too," I quipped.

My dad stood aside and pointed a stern finger in the general direction of the front door.

Great. I'd already been kicked out of my mom's house, and now I was being kicked out of my dad's. At least in this situation I'd be allowed to come back . . . probably.

I followed Chase down the hall toward the front door, trailing my fingers along the freshly repainted walls as I went. A few weeks prior I had practically destroyed my dad's house by making a portal. My grandmother was the only other known demon with the skill, but she didn't leave destruction in her wake. I was strictly banned from portal making until we could figure out what I was doing wrong.

I'd destroyed my mom's house too, but my dad assured me that the damages had been repaired. I'd probably never get to see for myself if the house was okay. My throat tightened at the thought. I knew the events in my life were difficult for my loved ones to cope with, but I never thought I'd see the day when my mom couldn't bear to be near me. I knew she was just afraid, but that knowledge didn't make it any easier for me to deal with.

Chase helped me into my well-worn, brown leather jacket (a hand-me-down from Allison), to cover up the soft white tee shirt I was wearing, then put on his faded green, military style jacket. It would be cold outside because it was still snowy back in Shelby, and the demon underground tended to mirror the weather in the real world. Still, a few months ago I would have been fine going out into the cold in my light-weight, hunter green tee shirt, but my demon hot-flashes had finally settled down.

I breathed in the cool air as we stepped outside and started walking. The exact mechanics of why it was currently cold in the underground still confused me, but I'd learned that the demon world was actually a parallel plane to the world of humans, like if the earth had a vast underground cave system filled with demons. Only, if you dug down in the real world, the demons wouldn't actually be there. You couldn't see humans from the underground, and humans couldn't see demons unless someone summoned one of us. The whole summoning thing was another confusing convention that I didn't quite understand.

Besides summoning, the only other way for full-blooded demons to see the human world was portals. Portals could allow full demons to travel above ground, or to any other realms for that matter, without all of the pesky drawbacks of summoning. Without portals, only those with a portion of human blood running through their veins could go to the human world, and even then only a few of them had the power to do so. My dad was one such demon. I, on the other hand, was currently stuck unless my dad sent me up, or I wanted to destroy his house again. We really needed to figure out the problem with my portals.

Chase grabbed my sleeve and pulled me aside as I nearly walked right into a mailbox. Yes, demons get mail too.

"Did you just venture off into Xoe land again?" Chase asked jokingly.

I'd been spacing out a lot lately. I couldn't help it. I had a lot on my mind.

"Where do you think Jason went?" I asked distantly for the billionth time.

Chase shrugged as we continued walking. "He's a big, scary vampire, Xoe. He can take care of himself."

I looked down at my sneakers as we walked. "I know. I just don't understand why he left. You'd think he could have at least written me a letter so I would know what's going on."

Chase sighed. We'd had this conversation many times before. "He'll come back."

I glanced over at Chase as we walked, feeling guilty for making him listen to my incessant whining about Jason, when he was probably the last person that wanted to hear it. He'd finally cut his black hair, and it was now short enough that you could barely tell how wavy it could be. My pale blonde hair fell limply past my shoulders, longer than I'd had it in years.

I wanted to ask Chase if he thought that Jason had somehow found out about our kiss, but I bit my tongue. I still didn't know what the kiss meant to me, and I was *so* not ready to talk about it with Chase. He'd let the whole thing go regardless. I'd been delirious with blood-loss, and he had saved my life. End of story.

We reached the steps of the large, gold-brick library and sat down side-by-side. The library's front steps had become our regular hangout since I'd been banished to the underworld. It was probably a strange place to choose, since we'd killed Chase's ex-girlfriend behind the building, but I liked it anyhow.

I leaned my shoulder against Chase's and watched the demons as they walked by. Most looked like normal humans, but there was the occasional red pair of eyes, or set of full-body scales mixed in with the crowd. No one paid us much mind, which was a comforting feeling in its own right. Sometimes it was nice to feel invisible.

My phone buzzed obnoxiously in my jacket pocket, disturbing the peaceful moment. It's strange, but I get perfect reception from most places in the underground. Maybe the demons had their own cell phone towers.

I checked my texts to see a new one from Allison. I almost ignored it, not feeling in the mood for talking, but went ahead and opened it. I could always just reply later.

The message read, "Hey Xoe, do you remember that girl Claire that was in our Biology class?"

I let out a huff of frustration, then replied facetiously, "Gee Allison, no hey, how are you doing? I know your mom disowned you and your boyfriend is missing, but what's important now is if you remember a girl named Claire."

I pushed send, then rolled my eyes at Chase as I waited for a reply.

My phone buzzed again and I looked down. "She's dead. She was murdered."

I paused for a few heartbeats, unsure of how to reply. I didn't actually remember who Claire was, and now I felt awful for not remembering.

The phone buzzed again. "This feels weird to me, Xoe. Too much has happened."

The reply was cryptic as best, but I understood. It probably wasn't wise to admit over text that we had been involved in a few . . . disappearances. Nothing had come back to bite us yet, but a part of me was always waiting for the other shoe to drop.

"I'll try to come up," I replied finally.

My phone buzzed again almost instantly. "Good. I'll be home."

Chase watched my expression, worry clear in his dark gray eyes. "What's going on, Xoe?"

I smiled weakly at him. "Sometimes I forget that you don't just read texts over my shoulder like Allison and Lucy do."

"Um, sorry for not reading your personal conversations?" he offered.

I stood. "A girl was killed in Shelby, and Allison has a bad feeling about it . . . but when we ask my dad to send us up we're just going to say that I want to see Allison and Lucy. Deal?"

"Maybe we shouldn't-" he began, but I had already started walking.

I really wasn't being arrogant in thinking that this girl's murder somehow involved me and my twisted little world. There was at least a fifty-fifty chance . . . no, make that sixty-forty . . . seventy-thirty? I shook my head as I walked. A demon's work is never done.